HIDE AND SEEK

On the run, a serial killer lays a trap

DENVER MURPHY

THE
BOOK
FOLKS

Published by The Book Folks

London, 2019

© Denver Murphy

ISBN 978-1-7956-4646-8

www.thebookfolks.com

Hide and Seek is the second book in a trilogy featuring retired detective Jeffrey Brandt. Details about the other books can be found at the end of this one.

Prologue

The hotel room may have been unfamiliar to DCI Stella Johnson when she awoke, but she immediately knew where she was and how she had come to be there. The drugs provided by the staff at the hospital were still helping to numb her physical pain, but nothing could dull the anguish she was experiencing.

A mere 48 hours ago she had never felt more alive, being tantalisingly close to winning the two prizes she coveted most. In apprehending the serial killer who had been terrorising communities across the country, she would have passed the greatest challenge in her career, and could then focus on what she had been denying herself all this time: McNeil.

When news of the first stabbing in Nottingham reached the station, Johnson had been forced to collect someone from uniform to accompany her to interview their initial suspect. PC McNeil, still relatively new to the force and many years her junior, was only meant to be a makeweight. He was to be seen but not heard. And yet, long before she saw anything romantic there, it was clear he had the makings of a good detective.

When it became clear that they weren't just dealing with a one-off incident, she came to rely on McNeil's assistance. More than just an effective sounding board, his natural instincts were strong, and he had helped to stop her near-obsessive need to catch the killer from becoming too unorthodox in approach.

But that was until their quarry made the mistake of trying too hard to cover up a murder in which he had failed to take his actions to a new level of depravity.

Reverting back to his preferred method of stabbing his victims in the street, the man Johnson now knew to be former Detective Superintendent Jeffrey Brandt, had fooled everyone except her. Determined to use this to her advantage, she had sought to draw him out through a scurrilous newspaper article. McNeil only found out about her plan when he read the morning headlines, not only illustrating that she knew she had been crossing the line with this strategy, but also meaning that she was solely responsible for what happened next.

Casting aspersions of a sexual nature did bring Brandt out into the open but not in the way she had expected. He had lain in wait for her outside the police station and had followed her home with the intention of demonstrating to his accuser first hand that he was neither confused as to his sexuality, nor was he unable to become physically aroused by women.

Having punched Johnson into unconsciousness at her front door, he had stripped her and tied her to her bed. But the knowledge that he had ultimately been unsuccessful didn't bring the slightest shred of comfort to Johnson as she stared at her hotel room ceiling. She didn't know why McNeil had chosen to come around to her house that night, but there was no denying that they had become more than just colleagues. The thought that he had been unable to respect her calls for patience only served to cause Johnson more pain. The feelings he had developed for her – feelings that she had nurtured and

4

cultivated – may have ended up saving her, but in so doing McNeil had paid the ultimate price.

Chapter One

The sight of McNeil holding up the knife that only a moment ago was buried in his chest, caused the screams of protest to die in Johnson's throat. She continued to stare at him as he delicately placed it in her hands.

She didn't want it; all she wanted was him.

Allowing it to drop onto the bed, she grasped his hand instead. His look of regret was replaced with a smile. But it soon faded along with their connection, despite Johnson clutching him with all her might. His eyes remained steady but were no longer focused on her. Fear overcame her once more and the screaming recommenced.

Johnson didn't want to let go of McNeil, as though the very act would cause him to be lost. The calls for him to wake up mutated into unintelligible screeching; a sound so alien that it endangered her sanity. But amidst the wild panic there remained a single shred of coherence. If he were to be saved, she would need help. Releasing his hand and severing their physical bond was the hardest thing she had ever done. With her grip now free, she frantically scrabbled around, horrified that the knife might have fallen to the floor. So relieved was she to feel the metal blade that she grabbed it, cutting herself in the process. Working her fingers along to the hilt, she contorted her wrist in an attempt to hack her bonds. She missed, and the jarring of metal upon metal as she gouged the wrought-iron bed frame, almost caused the knife to slip out of her slick palm. Gripping it to the extent that she heard her knuckles crack, she tried again and, with a few rough strokes, her hand became free. Fighting the pins and needles in her arm, she managed to twist herself, allowing her to tackle the other side. Johnson relied on her core strength to haul herself up into a sitting position, so she could attend to her feet, not caring that her desperate slashes left gashes on her ankles.

Resisting the urge to leap from the bed and sweep McNeil up in her embrace, she made her way unsteadily to the door, using the wall for support. Desperation drove her on and, despite her injuries, she took the stairs two at a time. With only thoughts of McNeil in her mind, the body spread across the floor at the bottom nearly caused her to lose her balance as she abruptly came to a halt. Before her was the man responsible for this atrocity; lying in a pool of his own blood. A wave of revulsion surged through her, only to be replaced by pride that McNeil had risked his life to save her. She wondered why he had come to her house, given they had agreed to part for the evening, and remembered her appeal in the police station car park for him to be patient and to allow their investigation to take precedence- – the knowledge that their relationship would be unprofessional mixing with her usual sense of panic that she was letting someone into her life. She cursed herself for refusing to deal with the strength of her feelings; she had known he liked her but had been scared that it was merely a crush on an older woman. If him choosing to come around, despite what she had said, was not enough to convince her otherwise, then what he did upstairs, so willingly and tenderly, showed she had been wrong to fear her feelings.

Thoughts of McNeil's sacrifice served to rouse Johnson from her regrets and focus on the immediate. She wanted revenge for all the pain and suffering this disgusting creature in front of her had caused. It mattered not that he was dead; she would derive satisfaction from repeatedly slamming her bare heel onto his skull until it was crushed beyond all recognition. The nakedness he had inflicted on her would no longer be part of his act of degradation; disrobed she would be better able to revel in her obliteration of his physical form.

But that would have to wait.

McNeil was all that mattered, and she would resist her primeval need for retribution in order to save him. Carefully stepping over the body to avoid slipping in the dark pool of blood that glistened in the evening light, she scouted round for her handbag; silently cursing its absence. Knowing that she was wasting precious seconds, Johnson rushed into the sitting room to retrieve the house phone from its charging point.

Despite her line of work, this was the first time she had dialled 999 and was initially confused when her call was answered by an operator asking which service she required. Acknowledging the priority, she demanded an ambulance. When this was met with an enquiry as to the nature of the emergency, she found herself ranting about a serial killer and her boyfriend lying stabbed upstairs. Whatever she said must have worked because the calm and professional tone that had greeted her, was now alarmed but managing to inform her that a medical team had been dispatched using the address her number was linked to. Johnson was told she would need to hold the line whilst being transferred to the police.

'Just fucking get them here!' She shouted, throwing the handset down without ending the call; she needed to get back upstairs. The thought of McNeil just lying there, injured and alone, was unbearable and dizziness threatened to collapse her. She grasped the mantelpiece and tried to bring her breathing under control. As well as her vision, she could feel her sense of logic begin to restore and recognised that she would need to be able to open the front door if she didn't want to risk having to leave McNeil again when the ambulance arrived. It was with this intention that she exited the sitting room, only to be met with the rush of air and added brightness signalling someone already had.

Chapter Two

There is a sound that punctuates the nothingness. Faint at first but gradually building until it becomes unmistakable. Screams. Are they his own? That would certainly account for the pain he is feeling but, as they continue, they don't sound like him. He should open his eyes and get up but he's afraid. Not just of whatever is making that inhuman screeching – he also senses that the pain is only going to intensify if he allows his body to fully regain consciousness. He has an overwhelming urge to give in to the temptation to slip under again, where there is no sound, no feeling – just warm, blissful oblivion. He must have; he can no longer hear anything. But, even if it were not for the physical discomfort he is still experiencing, he shouldn't be thinking anything now.

The decision whether to wake or sleep remains. His body is demanding that it is allowed time to rest and repair, but his mind is telling him he is in danger. He doesn't know what from, and if it has anything to do with the owner of those screams. His mind is fractured though, with another part of it imploring him to fade away and abandon an agony that goes far beyond whatever injuries he has just sustained.

'Just hold on, I'll get help.' It isn't so much the words themselves that end the conflict within his immobile form, but the tremendous power and intent with which they are delivered. The part of him that warns against returning to a life of misery must be wrong because this voice conveys a love that can conquer all obstacles. He will hold on to that and wait for the assistance that will follow.

Whether it is just moments or hours later is unclear, for time is different where he currently resides. That voice has returned but it being nearer isn't the only difference. The desperation remains but the warmth has gone. She, for it is now undoubtedly female, is shouting about an attack. Has he been attacked? Is that why he is here? He can't believe that she is the cause of his pain, not when she spoke to him with such passion. They must know each other; a fact confirmed by the familiarity of the voice. Is she his wife? He vaguely remembers being married but can't identify her name or anything about her.

'Just fucking get them here!' The change in tone fully awakened Brandt. He knew exactly who it belonged to and the immediate, massive dump of adrenaline in his system opened his eyes. Ignoring the thudding in his head, he rose to his feet. He started to move in her direction but paused as he slipped and nearly lost his balance. Beneath him was an alarmingly large pool of blood and an instinctive raise of his hand to the back of his head revealed it was his. The pain from earlier returned and multiplied. He didn't know where his knife was, and he understood that the help Johnson had promised was going to be in the form of the authorities.

Brandt turned towards the door and flung it open. Greeted by the cool evening air, it refreshed his face and brought a welcome hit of oxygen. He banished the idea that he should stay and finish the job and stumbled onto the front pathway and out of the gate. If he could just make it to his car and get away from here, he could give his body the respite it was demanding. He had no idea of

11

the response times in this area but if the police believed she was still in danger they would rush here as quickly as possible.

But the risk of capture was no longer his immediate concern.

The noise from behind caused him to look around and he staggered to the side and into a parked car. Johnson, naked except for a small pair of black panties, was flying out of her front door. The sight terrified him and there was no notion of standing his ground. There was a savagery to her features that added to the shrieking and Brandt was certain that, should she catch him, he would be torn limb from limb.

He pushed himself upright, not noticing that it was her car that had saved him from falling, and lurched the final few metres to his own vehicle. With the distance between them closing the whole time it was only the fact he hadn't locked his door that saved Brandt. He pulled it open as Johnson rounded the bonnet and, seeing the hatred and fury in her eyes, he swung his feet into the car before she ran into the door without slowing her pace. She bounced off it, the effect of which caused it to slam shut. Brandt immediately reached to lock it before she could start yanking on the handle. He still hadn't retrieved the key from his pocket, but his more immediate concern was the car's lack of central locking. He reached across to secure the passenger side but was stopped by the loud thud from his own window. He turned and looked in horror to see Johnson's arm pulled back to make another attempt to smash the glass. Brandt could hear his own screams as a rock, clutched by her fist, slammed inches from his face. The smear of blood left from cuts on her hand stirred him into action once more. Overwhelming relief at, not only finding the key immediately upon thrusting his hand into his pocket, but also managing to pull it out and insert it into the ignition without dropping it, was abruptly ended by Johnson's next swing disintegrating the window.

Brandt was showered with glass an instant before her bloodied hand reached in to claw at his features. Instinctively turning his head away from the danger, he roared in pain as her nails dug at the wound from earlier. Twisting the key, he heard the familiar sound of the starter motor turning over but failing to fire, soon to be drowned out by Johnson's screams. Her claws had turned into fists once more and she was now punching his head. The sustained shocks to his brain were causing his vision to close and Brandt knew he wouldn't be able to withstand her fury much longer. It was only when the punches stopped that he realised the engine had somehow caught and was now idling roughly. He risked turning his face to look at Johnson, whose expression revealed the dawning horror that he may escape. He slammed it into first gear, looked up and saw her throw herself on the bonnet and use the windscreen wipers to prevent herself falling off.

The car in front was pared close to him and, without the aid of power steering, he caught the blue Fiesta as he attempted to pull out into the road. The contact wasn't sufficient to dislodge Johnson who, not only remained on the bonnet, but was repositioning herself so she could hold on with just her left hand, freeing her right to attack the windscreen. Brandt doubted that she would be able to break through but wasn't prepared to find out. With her fist now raised he decided against changing gear and built up more speed. With the engine bouncing off the rev limiter he slammed on the middle pedal instead. At that moment he fully intended to dislodge Johnson and then proceed to drive over her but what his pikey piece of shit car gave with one hand by starting, it took with the other. The unnerving but now familiar sensation of the uneven brakes making the car lurch to the right as the wheels locked, did cause Johnson to be thrown from the vehicle but across to the other side of the road. Now stationary, Brandt would have to back up if he was going to find the angle necessary to hit her. As he automatically checked his

13

rear-view mirror before putting the car in reverse, he could see the blue of flashing lights in the murky gloom of dusk behind him. Even the few seconds it would take to complete his manoeuvre might be enough for him to be spotted.

Reluctantly placing the lever back in first, he resisted the temptation to see if he might manage enough steering lock to get her, knowing that a car pitching onto the other side of the road would be far more noticeable and, notwithstanding the immediate danger that would place him in, the last thing he wanted was to point out where Johnson lay.

As he took off up the road, he hoped that the impact of the hard tarmac on her soft, naked body had been enough to finish the job.

Chapter Three

The shrill ringtone awoke DSI Franklin with a start. The room appeared different from when he first slumped on his sofa; the bright late spring sunshine having been replaced by night. Although his hangover remained, it was far less potent than before, and he didn't regret making the excuse to leave the office early, so he could return home.

Not yet anyway.

'Boss, where are you?'

'I'm out in the field following up a lead.' Detective Superintendent Franklin knew that his team only respected him because of his position of authority. Much as they tried to hide it, the slight shaking of heads and unwitting roll of eyes that greeted a number of his key decisions revealed this. Other people with his status may not have noticed, much less cared, but it was his emotional intelligence that had got him so far. His police work had been solid at best, but he'd risen through the ranks from an ability to be in the right place at the right time, as well as a willingness to seek credit for the actions of others. It was only natural when a superior moved on for there to be some jockeying for position, but Franklin had maintained an advantage by anticipating things long before they happened. He liked to build up networks of contacts so that he could sense the way the wind was blowing; well in advance of a decision being made. He had become skilled at knowing the right time to brown nose certain people and when to disassociate himself from others.

Even with his retirement looming, he still longed for one final step up. It wasn't just that being DSI wasn't sufficiently elevated to satisfy his ambitions, the position itself was an awkward balancing act between managing those on the ground and fulfilling the demands from above. If he could just join the top brass, then he wouldn't have to deal directly with pricks like DC Pulford calling him. Instead he would only then have to harry DSIs, in much the way he had been badgered over the years. Demanding results would be much easier than having to deliver them. But, try as he might, and despite using every political trick he had honed over his career, he had been unsuccessful in getting that leg up. Whereas some of the DSIs whom he had befriended walked into promotions after only a token year or two in the job and, worse still, others refused requests for them to apply, Franklin had always found himself blocked.

He knew his increasing frustration at having to remain in a post that he neither wanted nor was particularly good at, was a contributing factor in the breakdown of his marriage. It wasn't the sole cause and, when his wife had confessed to falling out of love with him, it shouldn't have come as such a shock given he had never loved her in the first place. He had approached relationships in the same calculated way as his career. By his early thirties he felt that having a family would give the impression of stability and dependability; allowing him to adorn his desk with the sort of photos that his superiors felt necessary to demonstrate their humanity whilst delivering tough decisions.

Franklin had chosen his partner carefully; neither attractive enough to be considered a trophy wife and provoke jealousy from others, nor sufficiently unappealing as to lower his credibility among the men of the force. That she was career driven helped because the additional money had come in handy, and it meant she didn't complain about his long hours. They had taken expensive holidays together and had been able to send their two children to independent school. But with them growing up and more interested in social media than having a conversation with their father, and Franklin using alcohol more frequently to anaesthetise him from the increasingly frustrating days at work, he and his wife had grown apart.

What he needed was one high profile case, one that was firmly rooted in the public domain, where the credit he would take for cracking it would make his next application impossible to ignore. Perhaps then he could focus on winning his wife back and spend his retirement learning how to love her.

Franklin had observed the events unfolding in Nottinghamshire with a growing sense of injustice, which only intensified when the murderer decided to move on to Kent. When it finally came to his patch, he could barely conceal his delight. Not only was it all over the national newspapers, but his solving of something two other constabularies had failed to do was certain to see the top brass begging for him to join them.

Except he hadn't been able to solve it. The attack in Milton Keynes appeared as random as the others.

'Look, what is it?' He demanded grumpily.

'There's been another attack.'

Franklin didn't need to know who the caller was referring to. 'Here?'

'No, guv, back in Nottingham.'

'Fuck!' He had known the DSI there for a number of years and knew he played with a straight bat. He would follow protocol and share the necessary information, but Franklin didn't like that the limelight would be shifting back to him. He'd very much enjoyed taking the central position in the recent press conference and had viewed

Potter playing second fiddle as handing him the baton. 'When? I need details!'

'If you were here you would know that…'

'You mind your tone! I've already told you that I'm following up something important!' Franklin made a mental note to ensure that Pulford's next leave request found some spurious reason not to be granted. Perhaps an office reshuffle that saw him moved to just outside the toilets would also be in order.

'Sorry, guv,' Pulford said without sounding even the least bit remorseful. 'Is it the guy from the email?'

'What?' Franklin had no idea what he was referring to.

'You know, the image of the suspect we were sent earlier.'

'Yes, that's the one.' He didn't like how unconvincing he sounded and, although he still needed the details from Pulford, knew he should end this call as soon as possible. 'Look, I'm just finishing up here. I'll be with you in half an hour.' He hung up without waiting for reply, in a petulant attempt to reassert his authority.

Franklin immediately opened his work emails on his phone. As soon as he found out what the hell Pulford was going on about, he would jump in his car and get back to the station. He might even call Potter on his way to see if he could get the information straight from the horse's mouth. It would also serve as a reminder that he wasn't going to be cut out of the loop on this one.

There it was, at the bottom of the list of all the various messages he had been sent over the past few hours. He didn't bother reading the contents and went straight for the attached image.

His mouth opened to laugh at the grainy CCTV-derived still, so indistinct as to demonstrate the desperation on the part of those who sent it. But no sound emerged from Franklin. Even on the small screen of his smartphone, there was no doubt in his mind who this person was.

It was Jeff. It was his friend and colleague of many years, former Detective Superintendent Jeffrey Brandt.

'Fucking hell,' Franklin whispered. With his mind unable to process the implications of what he had viewed, he reverted back to the body of the email. There it was in black and white. The man in the photo, having been seen on cameras around some of the locations, and at times consistent with when the murders had taken place, was wanted for questioning.

Whilst Franklin remained certain that the image was undoubtedly of Brandt, he couldn't believe that his friend would somehow be involved. What was troubling him most was that he had been sent this hours earlier, and for him not to have noticed that it was the man whom he had spent the whole of the previous day with would, at the very least, make him seem incompetent.

'Shit!' What made matters worse was that Franklin had just told DC Pulford that he had been following this up for the last few hours. He needed to think and to think fast. Perhaps if he could get to Brandt first, not only could he cover up his own mistake of leaving work early and not checking his messages but, by proving Nottingham had the wrong guy, he could discredit Potter's team in the process. A sound plan and one that could see him coming out of this smelling of roses.

A telephone conversation was likely to be awkward and it wouldn't explain his lengthy absence from the office; he would need to go around to Brandt's house and talk to him man to man. Quickly rushing into the kitchen to splash some water on his face and to sort out his hair, flattened at the back whilst he had been asleep, he grabbed his coat and headed out to his car.

Chapter Four

Initially sure that either he or the car would fail on some part of the journey, it was with relief he arrived back in his home town. Once Brandt had made it to the motorway, despite his head still throbbing, he spent the remainder of the time thinking through his options. There were many variables to consider but the upside was it drove any drowsiness from his mind. The first thing of concern was whether he was in immediate danger. It felt like there was a more than even chance Johnson had survived her fall, and he was grateful that he had at no point shared his identity with her. However, he was troubled by the look she had given him when he first approached. Beneath the initial shock he was sure there was some form of recognition and no matter how much he tried to reassure himself that he must have misinterpreted her expression at a time of high emotion, he had learned long ago to trust his instincts.

Nevertheless, even if, for some reason, she had recognised him, Brandt was sure she didn't know his name. If she did it was game over anyway because that would mean she also knew his address and the police would be waiting for him back at his house. Even if it wasn't for the need to go home and collect his money, fleeing altogether now would clearly leave the issue of the car. It didn't matter that it was unlikely she noticed the number plate, a simple description of the vehicle either by her, or one of the neighbours who must have been alerted by the commotion outside, would be sufficient. How long it would take to track would depend on the quality of the description and the proximity of the nearest camera. Once they were able to establish the registration, they could then use the various ANPRs to trace his route. If they knew who he was, without any money, he wouldn't get far.

If, as was far more likely, his name was yet unknown, then the car wasn't too much of a concern because it had always been part of the plan for him to dump it. One of the key reasons why he had bought one of those he found advertised on a verge, in this case sold by a traveller, was so that it would be extremely hard to trace it back to him. Even if his encounter with Johnson had gone smoothly, the knowledge that officers' personal details were carefully guarded would have led to the assumption that she had been followed from the police station. It would not have taken them long to work out which vehicle was involved. The spot would be sufficiently far from the nearest camera and suitably secluded to take the police some time to find it. Moreover, even once they did, it would be far enough from Brandt's home to provide no likely link.

But things hadn't gone smoothly. With all the other variables, Brandt thought he couldn't afford the subsequent four-mile walk and would have to risk bringing the car much closer to home to give him sufficient time to collect what he needed and make his escape. He settled on a location a mile or so beyond his house, knowing they would assume he had stopped short of his destination instead.

It was with a slight tinge of regret that he got out of his vehicle. It had fought the odds of its low price and dubious provenance to provide him with reliable transport, notwithstanding its multitude of faults. It would never be driven again, all that awaited it was to be trailered somewhere to be forensically analysed before finding itself sent to the crusher. As he set off on foot, Brandt hoped the car's certain future wasn't a metaphor for his own.

The relatively short journey seemed to take an age but, even if it had not been for fear of worsening the pain in his head, he didn't want to draw attention to himself by rushing. With the clouds obscuring the light from the moon, so that the blood on his clothes was barely visible, he hoped to any observers that he would appear to be a middle-aged man doing nothing more sinister than walking home from the pub.

As soon as Brandt entered his street, he used his trained eyes to establish there was no one staking out his house. This also meant it was highly unlikely that there would be anyone inside waiting for him, but he still felt trepidation as he opened his front door.

All was exactly how he had left it.

Chapter Five

Johnson was in Canterbury. She was in the hotel lift and McNeil was kissing her. She wanted to wait until she got him into her room but could not resist his soft open mouth and probing tongue. Fiercely kissing him in return, she looped her hand round the back of his head, so she could draw him in closer. She wanted her whole body in contact with him and her arousal became heightened by the feeling of his erection digging into her.

The ping of the lift to announce its arrival at their floor was an unwelcome interruption but as she pulled away, she could see her disappointment reflected in McNeil's face. She laughed; she couldn't help herself. This is what she had wanted for some time now and she was only moments away from getting it. As soon as she had decided to go to Canterbury and inspect the body, she knew there was a chance that this would happen. She hadn't wanted to rush it, not least because she hadn't been sure that McNeil wanted it too. So, she had conspired to ensure they stayed overnight and spent just enough time buying the right clothes and applying the right make up so that he would forget the age gap and the challenges that they would face keeping it a secret at work.

And yet he hadn't displayed the impetuousness of youth; appearing content instead to visit some of Canterbury's pubs, each one as lifeless as the last. Having consumed enough wine, Johnson found the courage to make her move. But even then, as they had walked back to the hotel, she wasn't sure it was what he wanted until she saw the look of anguish on his face when she cruelly led him to believe that her suggestion of room service had been entirely innocent.

'Your place or mine?'

Johnson knows the confidence of the question is belied by the nervousness of his tone. But he has every right to be nervous because she has planned this to the nth degree, and he is going to get the workout of his life.

'Mine, definitely mine.'

She pauses by her door, searching for her key card. She needs to remove the obstacle of her phone, so she can look for it properly. She is about to hand it to McNeil but a voice in her head screams for her not to. It tells her to forget the fucking key card and use his bed instead. But she had spent a lot of time getting her room ready and, besides, she doesn't like being told what to do, even by her own consciousness. What's so wrong with asking him to hold her phone anyway? It's not as though there's anything on there that he shouldn't see.

But there is something on there that he shouldn't see. Not only does Johnson know exactly what's on there but she also understands why she knows. This isn't happening. Some of it did happen but she's not in Canterbury anymore.

* * *

She woke up in a room she had never seen before, but her surroundings instantly informed her of where she was. The process of lifting her left arm to observe the drip being fed into her via the cannula on the back of her hand, took tremendous effort. Looking back up the tube she could see it split between saline solution and something much smaller which she guessed to be morphine or some other potent pain relief.

It was consideration of the various aches she could feel throughout her body that caused her to recollect how she got there. Johnson recalled arriving home to be interrupted on her doorstep. That moment of recognising the man from the CCTV images the instant before she saw the swing of his fist. She had been too late to react and had woken naked, bar her pants, and tied to her bed. Then he was crawling over her, releasing his erection from his trousers. She remembered him biting her nipple and could instantly feel the discomfort of her breast once more. Then there was the crash of her front door and the struggle between McNeil and her attacker. The sickening thumps of the two bodies falling down the stairs before McNeil staggered back to her. Johnson screwed her eyes shut in an attempt to block what came next and reached behind her to find the alarm.

Moments later a nurse rushed in. 'Oh gosh, you're awake. Here, let me turn this up a bit for you.' She was reaching for the smaller of the two drip liquids.

'No, no!' Johnson bellowed, unable to stretch enough to intercept her. 'Don't you fucking touch that!'

The force of her command caused the nurse to stop. She stared, frightened, into Johnson's wild eyes.

'McNeil, where is he?'

The nurse remained motionless, transfixed. 'I don't kn… know who you mean,' she stammered after a few moments.

'McNeil,' she cried. 'The man who would have been brought in with me.'

The nurse didn't respond but the look of horror on her face was sufficient as an answer.

Johnson's screams brought the police officer stationed outside her room charging in. His initial panic was halted by the nurse shouting: 'Don't just stand there, hold her down!'

Johnson managed to catch him with a wild flail of her right arm before he launched himself onto the bed in an effort to pin her down. The feeling, so reminiscent of being straddled by that sick bastard earlier, caused her to buck and writhe and thrash all the more. She barely noticed the cool sensation of the fluid being pumped through the cannula and directly into her blood stream, but a few moments later she could feel her strength draining. At the same time, the body on top of her began to get lighter and the fury that drove her was replaced by calmness.

'Thank fuck for that,' the officer murmured, unsure whether it was now safe to get up.

'I think we'd better strap her down before she wakes again,' the nurse said, laughing nervously.

Chapter Six

The knock at the door made Brandt instantly freeze. He was in the process of feeding the magazine into his Glock 17 pistol, having been at home a matter of minutes and, following a quick change of clothes, having shoved some items into a small holdall and retrieved the shoebox full of money from under his bed.

His senses were on high alert and he could feel the adrenaline coursing through his veins as he rammed the clip home before sliding the top back to put a round in the chamber, in the same manner as the man in north London had shown him a few days earlier. Checking the safety was still on, he crept towards the window, wincing as one of the floor boards squeaked under him. He didn't expect to see a fleet of police cars outside; if nothing else for the fact that, if there was, they wouldn't be knocking. What Brandt did see, bathed in the harsh white of the security light he had installed many years earlier, was a BMW X5 SUV perched at the end of his drive.

As far as he was aware, he didn't know anyone with such a vehicle and his instincts were screaming out that it was too much of a coincidence for this to be unrelated to his actions that afternoon.

Another knock, louder and more insistent on this occasion, interrupted Brandt's attempt to make sense of this. It couldn't be someone going door to door at this time of night but the urge to remain upstairs in the hope that whoever it was would go away was strong.

'Jeff it's me!' Came the call from below. Brandt started to wonder how this person knew his name when comprehension suddenly dawned.

He didn't know why Franklin had chosen to visit him but knew it would seem odd if he wasn't in at this time on a Monday night. Perhaps he had called earlier and was concerned that Brandt hadn't answered. Given what a state he had got himself into yesterday maybe he had assumed the same of Brandt and took his apparent absence as something having befallen him.

Whatever it was, he wanted to get rid of him quickly, even if a small part of Brandt would enjoy the look on that career hungry prick's face if the specialist firearms unit came bursting in. 'Just a moment, Brian, I was on the loo.' He shouted down, going into the en-suite to flush the toilet for effect. He wedged the Glock into the waistband of his trousers as he had seen done in countless American films, but the object felt so alien there. A quick glance in the full length mirror his wife had spent so long staring into before she left, confirmed that there was a definite bump under his shirt. He considered tucking it into the back instead but that wouldn't address his concern about it falling out, especially if he ended up sitting down. Instead he tossed it on the bed next to the shoebox and used the duvet to cover up both items.

'Brian!' Brandt called cheerfully as he opened the front door, before the expression on Franklin's face caused him to change his approach. 'Is something the matter?'

'Do you mind if I come in, Jeff?'

'No, not at all,' Brandt said, moving back into the hallway. 'Can I get you a drink or something?'

'Er, yeah sure,' he replied, devoid of any enthusiasm for what was being proposed.

Brandt was concerned. Franklin's odd behaviour was adding to the suspicions he held about the timing of his unsolicited visit. He moved to the drinks cabinet to buy himself an opportunity to think. Perhaps seeing whether he drank some of the whisky he was pouring would help to confirm whether he was here in some sort of official capacity. Then again, given the state Franklin had got into recently, Brandt doubted this would be the first time he had consumed alcohol whilst on the job.

'What's happened to the back of your head?'

Shit! Brandt had cleaned himself up when he got home but it was stupid of him to have let him see the wound. 'Oh, it's a little embarrassing really but I tripped over on the platform yesterday. I guess we overdid it a little.'

'Yeah,' Franklin gave a small laugh. 'You should really get it checked out though. Looks nasty.'

'I guess,' he replied, instantly grateful that Johnson hadn't managed to claw his face whilst he had been starting up the car. He walked over and handed Franklin the glass, noting the way he looked at its golden contents with an almost reverential longing. 'Is there something I can do for you Brian?'

Franklin took a long swig which Brandt appeared to replicate but, much as the heady aroma was appealing, he knew it was imperative he remain sharp. Yet he couldn't resist licking his lips to make the most of the liquid that had faintly brushed his mouth.

'What have you been up to this evening, Jeff?' The casual way it was delivered, under the pretence of small talk, was almost convincing but Brandt could read the intensity in Franklin's eyes. But tonight had been messy and he wanted to make as clean a getaway as possible, so he wouldn't act until he was certain.

'Ah, you know, this and that.'

'Like what exactly?' This was enough for Brandt. It wasn't so much the shift in tone but Franklin's need for specificity. It still didn't make sense though. Even if Franklin had been informed of what had happened to Johnson this evening, and had somehow managed to put two and two together based on the brief conversation they'd had about her in the pub after the Arsenal game yesterday, why come and face him alone? Franklin was a coward; of that Brandt was certain. So desperate was he to do the right thing in the eyes of his superiors that his averseness to risk had ensured he would never be considered for promotion. To come and face down a supposed dangerous killer was so completely out of character to be nonsensical.

'Well, I'm a little ashamed to say that I have been at the pub again this evening.' Giving a sheepish smile, he raised the whisky to his lips once more.

'Oh yeah, which one?'

Stupid fucking question. Franklin wasn't from round here. 'The Dog and Duck,' he replied, making up a name.

'Oh yeah, good was it?'

A seed of doubt was sown in Brandt's mind. Franklin was a pathetic specimen, of that he was certain. Perhaps he was just making inane conversation because he was lonely. Brandt's darkest days, those in which he had fantasised about plunging to his death, had usually started with a crushing hangover. There was no doubt Franklin was going through the same pain he had felt when his wife had left. He could imagine what today had been like because he had been through the same countless times whilst he was still in the force. You know everyone knows you're struggling with what's happened to you and so you try to hide it at work. This causes you to drink more when you're at home in order to either release all that pent-up feeling or to temporarily banish the misery, thus leading you to feeling worse at work which sees you going to even greater lengths to cover up the root of your misery and the resulting drink problem you've developed. Eventually it all gets too much, and you start considering the easy way out. The realisation that you are contemplating suicide can come as something of a shock and perhaps Franklin had just reached this point and decided to visit the only person he knew who may understand these feelings. But opening up is hard, certainly Brandt had never done it, so there was a possibility that Franklin was stumbling around trying to find other things to talk about.

'Yeah it was okay. Usual Monday quiz night.' The fact was, irrespective of Franklin's motives, Brandt couldn't spend all evening chatting shit. He needed to get away and the larger the gap he could get between him and his eventual pursuers, the greater his odds of escape. 'I hate to rush you Brian but I'm a little tired.'

'Okay, sure, sure.' Franklin said, nodding firmly. 'Look there was something specific I needed to talk to you about. It's about work…'

'I understand,' Brandt replied earnestly. 'You must have been feeling pretty rough this morning and I know it can be difficult trying to…'

'No, it's not that,' he interrupted impatiently. 'Well, it sort of is a bit, but something came through today from Nottingham…'

Brandt's heart froze in his chest. No more coincidences, no more bullshit thoughts about lonely coppers trying to come to terms with their wives leaving them. This was serious and he needed to get his gun. He needed to get his gun and find out exactly what Franklin was going on about and quickly. He needed to know exactly what Franklin knew and exactly what he had told anyone else. And then he needed to get out of here. Fast.

'Oh really?' Brandt asked, casually rising from his chair.

'Yeah, it's an image. Look, I've got it on my phone. It's probably nothing but I can't help but think the similarity is uncanny.' Franklin reached into his pocket and Brandt slowly walked across towards him. 'Here, let me show you...'

Now was the best opportunity Brandt was likely to get. He swept past Franklin. 'Hold on, I need to get my reading glasses.' He knew it sounded pathetic but anything to buy himself time.

'No, wait Jeff!' He called, following. 'You need to stay down here!' Whether it was the speed with which he was ascending the stairs that was causing alarm, Brandt didn't know, but he could hear Franklin just behind him. Any thoughts of the various aches and pains he had suffered that evening were gone; just the desperate need to reach his bedroom and get the gun. He felt a hand brush his heel in an attempt to trip him, but the contact wasn't sufficient, and he made it to the top knowing nothing could stop him covering the short distance across the landing to his bedroom. He flung back the duvet and grabbed the gun, swinging it immediately round to face Franklin.

But Franklin wasn't there.

A moment of confusion stunned Brandt before a dreadful realisation hit him.

'No, no!' he shouted, charging back towards the stairs. The front door was still closed, and he was sure he would have heard it if it had just been slammed shut. A loud thud from the back of the house revealed Franklin's whereabouts and Brandt followed the sound through the hallway and into the kitchen. He found Franklin there yanking on the French doors before trying again to smash his way out and into the garden.

Brandt switched on the light causing Franklin to instantly turn around. The look of sheer terror was almost comic. As he stared down at the mobile phone still in his hand, Brandt could see the faint glimmer of hope flash across his face. His thumb was already poised to dial 999 when Brandt flicked the safety off his Glock 17.

'If you don't drop that right now, I'm going to shoot you in the fucking face!'

That it fell to the floor without a moment's hesitation told Brandt all he needed to know about Franklin's likely compliance in what was to come.

'Right, let's have a little sit down again, shall we?'

If it wasn't for the gun in Brandt's hand, now resting casually on the arm of his chair, and the silent tears streaming down Franklin's face, anyone who hadn't observed the past two minutes would have assumed they were still involved in their earlier conversation.

With his heart rate gradually returning to normal, Brandt was feeling remarkably calm. Better, in fact, than earlier when the confusion and suspicion had been swirling round his mind. He would be better still once he had established from Franklin exactly what the situation was.

'Okay, Brian, time is tight so I'm going to ask you some simple questions. You are going to provide some straightforward answers to these simple questions otherwise I am going to shoot out your knee caps.' For good measure Brandt waggled the gun in the direction of Franklin's legs. 'But a quick word of warning before we start. If I even suspect you aren't telling me the truth, or are trying to hold something back, I'm going to shoot you in the stomach and I will sit here drinking the rest of my whisky whilst watching you bleed out. Clear?'

A resigned nod indicated Franklin was ready.

'Question one: does anyone else know you are here?'

'No.'

'Why are you here?'

'A photo came through of you on CCTV.'

This made lots of questions occur to Brandt but, for now, he just needed to stick to the important ones. 'But why are you here?'

'I wasn't sure it was you and er…'

'Go on…' Brandt could see there was something else to Franklin's answer, but he was struggling to phrase it.

'Well I, er, missed it. I had gone home to get some sleep and then I was called, and I had to…'

'Woah there!' he interrupted, holding up his free hand. 'I get it. Something about you being an incompetent prick.' He smirked at the hurt in Franklin's eyes. 'Does anyone know the person in the photo is me?' Already his mind was starting to wonder if this was the reason why Johnson had given him that look when he first arrived.

'Well, er, no, I don't think so. It's pretty grainy and I think it's only because we're friends that I was able...'

Brandt let out a loud and cruel laugh. 'Friends!? You dumb cunt! We're not friends. I just needed you, so I could get some information.' The look of confusion on Franklin's face came as a surprise. 'Don't you know where I've been this evening?'

He slowly shook his head. 'I was told there had been another attack in Nottingham, but...'

'You could say that. Thanks to you I visited a certain DCI Stella Johnson.' His voice was dripping with glee.

'But I don't know... how could I have...?'

'You really don't remember do you? After I got you legless in the pub yesterday, I used your indiscretion to get what I needed. I had hoped for more, but you gave me just enough.' He sat back enjoying a fresh wave of horror cross Franklin's face. 'One could say you are responsible for what happened,' he sniggered, ramming the point home.

'Is she... is she dead?'

'Who knows?!' Brandt shrugged, hiding the irritation he felt at being reminded he hadn't completed the job properly. 'I left her naked in the road, so your guess is as good as mine.' Long moments passed as he sat there thinking. 'Okay then, it's safe to assume no one else knows it's me,' he continued, more to himself this time. 'But then again, it won't take long now until the connection is made.'

He rose and gestured with an upwards motion of the gun that Franklin was to do the same. He remained on the sofa.

'What... what are you going to do to me?'

Brandt laughed again. 'I'm not going to do anything to you. As you said, we're old friends,' he mocked. 'We're just going on a little drive, that's all.'

'What? Where?'

'Now, now,' he shushed him. 'First things first, we need to retrieve your phone and switch it off. Then we need to head upstairs and collect the rest of my things. Oh, and there are a couple of items I have to get from the shed. I'm sure I don't need to remind you, do I, of what will happen if you try anything?'

* * *

A few minutes later they were in the BMW X5, Franklin at the wheel and Brandt sat diagonally behind him resting the gun in his gloved hands on his lap. Brandt had been happy to find that the rear windows were tinted. All the same, he was anxious now to get moving. His unexpected, and initially unwelcome, visitor had solved the problem of how to make his getaway, but until they were clear from his street he wouldn't feel at all comfortable.

'Off we go now, let's take it nice and steady.'

'Where are we going?'

'Your place of course,' he said casually, as though this was the most natural thing in the world. When the anticipated reaction of surprise didn't follow, Brandt repositioned himself, so he had a clearer line of fire. Franklin might be a pussy, but he was a devious bugger and he took his lack of a response as him plotting something. He didn't know what it was, but he had expected, once the shock of the situation wore off, that Franklin wouldn't remain quite as biddable as he had been whilst they had sat in the living room.

They remained in silence for most of the journey, save for the few questions Brandt asked in order to find out more about the origin of the CCTV image. Although he was frustrated that someone had managed to find the needle in the haystack, it was with a source of pride he noted that it had not come from any specific mistake on his part. Once satisfied that Franklin had no further information of value, he settled back to contemplate the details of his improvised strategy. That it also left Franklin to his own thoughts wasn't too much of a worry because, as soon as this stop-off was complete, he could proceed to the next part of his plan without concern.

'Just pull up outside and switch the lights off,' Brandt instructed when they arrived at Franklin's house. 'Nice place you've got there.'

He wasn't kidding. The large detached property was set back from the road and surrounded by neatly manicured hedges, save for the wrought iron gates that blocked the entrance to the gravel drive.

'Tell you what, when we're underway again you can tell me how someone on the same salary as me managed to bag himself such a decent pad.'

'We're going out again?' The surprise in his voice was evident. Brandt smirked at the implication that his plan had been to hide out indefinitely at a police officer's house.

'Even better than that, we're going on holiday,' he replied breezily. 'And what does everyone need when they go on holiday?'

'Erm, a suitcase?'

Brandt burst out laughing at the unintended humour. 'No Brian, they need their passport. Although if you're a good boy I will let you pack your Speedos.' He allowed his tone to immediately fall flat before continuing. 'As keen as I am for us to have a good time let me just remind you, I have killed many people before tonight and I won't hesitate for one moment…'

'Okay, okay!'

Brandt decided to let the interruption slide given the desperation contained within those two words. 'Just because you don't see the gun doesn't mean it's not about to blow your brains out. Final question before we get out: are we going to find anyone else in the house?'

'No.'

'Because you know what will happen to them…'

'No… I mean yes.'

'No wife deciding she can't live without you and come home? No children missing their Daddy and making a surprise visit?'

'No.' The bitterness in his voice was palpable.

'Great! I mean, not great. Actually, it's pretty sad, really…' Brandt corrected himself sarcastically.

'Fuck you, Jeff,' Franklin whispered.

'Ah come on, there's no need to be nasty, now is there?! Right, out you get.'

The two of them made their way slowly through the gates that had been opened using a remote control stored in the car's central console. The noise of their footsteps was loud against the quiet of the street and, despite having one himself, Brandt had to stifle a little shriek of surprise when the security light switched on automatically.

* * *

Perched on the end of the bed, carefully observing Franklin rummage through various drawers, Brandt wondered what was going through his mind right now. The mention of packing clothes had been an improvised joke, but Brandt had decided to run with it. He figured that the safest way to keep Franklin compliant was to give him hope. He knew all too well what people were capable of if they believed all to be lost. Even someone as spineless as Franklin might manage to get the jump on him if he thought there was no alternative, so affording him the time to pack a few clothes was a small price to pay for delaying that eventuality. Nevertheless, Brandt knew he would have to face this moment at some point if his plan were to be successful.

'Done?'

'Yes,' he said with a sigh.

'Mind if I check your passport?'

'Why?'

'Don't start making me all unhappy by becoming defensive. I just want to check you haven't popped an old one in by mistake.'

Franklin reluctantly handed it over. Although it was one way Brandt had anticipated that sneaky little bastard trying to put a spanner in the works, a quick examination of the cover, which was still intact without the snipped off corner, proved otherwise. 'Let me just check the dates,' he said opening up but only glancing to see that it had two years left. Instead his gaze lingered over the photograph.

'Just one more thing,' he added, getting up and handing the passport back to Franklin. 'Have you got your wife's address written down here somewhere?'

'What?' He shouted in shock. 'No. No, I don't.'

Brandt lifted up the gun in line with Franklin's navel. He closed one eye in a pretence at aiming. 'Remember what I said would happen if you lied to me?'

'What?' He repeated. 'I'm not lying.'

He raised the gun to his head, so he could look over the barrel and directly into his eyes.

'Yes, you are, Brian. What's more, if you don't tell me where it is right now, I'm going to shoot you in the head, find it, jump into that car of yours, go around to your wife's and shoot your kids in front of her.'

Brandt didn't intend any of this but could feel himself getting carried away with the power he held in his palm.

'And then I'm going to fuck her in front of her new boyfriend. She does have a new boyfriend, doesn't she? No, don't answer that! I don't want you to be upset. And then I'm going to kill her.' He paused, as though finished, enjoying Franklin's look of revulsion. 'But I'm going to let the boyfriend live,' he added finally.

Franklin remained there motionless and Brandt could see the conflict in his mind. He clearly believed every word he had been told and was wondering whether providing the address would lead to the same horrific outcome.

'Hey,' Brandt said in a lighter tone, eventually deciding to break the tension. 'Look, I'm sure your wife is sexy and everything, but we've got a holiday to get to and we can't afford any further delays.' He offered a reassuring smile. 'The address is just insurance, that's all, in case you try and do something stupid.'

The hope instantly returned to Franklin's pathetic face. 'You mean,' he croaked before using his tongue to wet his lips in an attempt to get the words out. 'You mean we're not going around there?'

'Course not. In case you hadn't noticed, I'm a wanted man and don't have time for affairs of the heart. Now grab that bag, let's get that address and we can hit the road.'

The contempt Brandt had always held for Franklin was continuing to multiply as he watched him virtually skip down the stairs in relief. He mused that it would be almost worth carrying out the threat of fucking his wife just to see his expression.

He was led into the kitchen; a huge open plan with gleaming marble worktops. Attached to the enormous American-style fridge freezer, among the various piss-poor drawings made by Franklin's kids when they were younger, was a scrap of white paper with an address on.

'You sure this is the one?' Brandt asked as it was handed to him, but the sadness with which Franklin regarded it meant that no answer was required. 'Right then, let's saddle up,' he said shoving it into his pocket.

Franklin had already made it to the hallway when the doorbell stopped them in their tracks. Barely a couple of seconds passed before it sounded again, only to be immediately followed by an impatient hammering on the door.

'Guv, it's me,' came the voice from outside.

'What have you done?' Brandt hissed, flicking the safety off the Glock once more, his mind desperately trying to work out when Franklin could have managed to call for help.

'Nothing, I swear!'

'Guv, I can see it's you.' His face was pressed against the small pane of frosted glass.

'Get rid of him!'

'What do you want Pulford?'

'Guv, I need to speak to you. When you didn't make it back to the station, I tried your phone…'

'Answer it but get him the fuck away. Quickly.' Brandt felt extremely uncomfortable watching Franklin walk slowly up the hallway. There were too many ways this could go wrong. 'Just remember I have your wife's address,' he called quietly after him.

'What do you want, Pulford?' Franklin repeated, pulling the door ajar. He hoped that the irritation in his voice, which had been easy to put on given how much he detested this pernicious little scroat, would be enough to stop Brandt from doing anything rash.

'Guv, we need you down at the station right now. There has been a development. Where were you by the way?'

'None of your fucking business.' It felt good to have a little power and control back. Now that Brandt knew where his wife and kids were, any thoughts of not doing exactly what he had been told were cast from his mind.

If DC Pulford was perturbed by his terse reply, he didn't show it. 'We've had a positive ID on the suspect.'

Franklin winced at the thought of Brandt hearing this and listened out for movement behind. His brain was screaming for him to barge past his visitor and get some distance. Pulford may be shot in the cross fire but that was okay as long as he made it to his car unharmed. He wondered whether he could get some officers round to his wife's house before Brandt got there. It was a mile or so up the road, but if he used Pulford's car…

'Guv, you alright?'

The question shook Franklin from his thoughts. 'So, who is it?'

'Well we don't know yet, guv, but it's the man from the image earlier.'

He let out a sigh of both frustration and relief. 'Well that's not a positive ID then, is it? You twat!'

'Well no, guv,' he replied, the hurt of which caused Franklin a brief moment of satisfaction. 'But they're cleaning up the images right now so that's why we need you back at the station.'

'Right, I'll follow you. I just need to lock up first.' Pulford remained stood there. 'Go on, fuck off then!' Franklin slammed the door and waited until the silhouette moved away from the glass. He turned around and gave a little yelp at the sight of Brandt who was now right behind him.

'Okay, good. We'll give it a minute and then you go out and check he's gone. I'll wait here with the gun trained on you.'

The time passed excruciatingly slowly for both of them. When Brandt finally indicated for him to go out, Franklin opened the door but then turned back. 'My bag?'

'Fuck your fucking bag,' Brandt hissed. 'I'll bring it out with me once we know the coast is clear.'

'I can't see,' he whispered before jumping up to look over the hedges that were obscuring his view. 'Shit!'

'What?'

'He's just waiting by his car.'

'Bollocks.' This was going horribly wrong. The moment the copper had mentioned identifying the suspect, Brandt had applied pressure to the trigger. He had waited for any movement from Franklin, even the slightest inclination of the head would have caused him to blow him away and then tackle his friend. The revelation that Pulford didn't have the first fucking clue what he was talking about, had stopped him doing so but Brandt regretted that now. 'Which way is he pointing?'

'What?'

'Which fucking way?'

'I… I don't understand…'

'The car you twat.'

'Oh, I see.' Franklin jumped again to find the answer to Brandt's question. The camp wave he provided Pulford, who had spotted him this time, might have been comic under other circumstances. 'The other way,' he said indicating left with his hand and in the opposite direction to where the X5 was facing.

Brandt wasn't comfortable with his hastily conceived plan, but time was of the essence and, in the absence of an alternative, it would have to do. 'Right, now go to your car and back into the drive so you can turn around to follow him.'

'I could probably just do a three-point turn in the road…'

'I know that,' Brandt said, exasperation causing his voice to be louder than intended. 'Just do it!'

'My bag?'

'I've got the sodding bag,' he spat, closing the door behind him. The security light was searingly bright, but he stayed low, walking on the grass alongside the driveway to avoid two sets of footsteps being audible. As they approached the gates he dashed to crouch behind the adjacent section of hedge. 'Just reverse in enough so that I can get in the back.'

Franklin didn't reply and walked out the gates, towards the X5. He turned around to give another wave to Pulford as well as a twirling gesture that he hoped would convey his intention to turn the car around. To the side he could see the crouched figure of Brandt, who had gained a clear line of sight all the way to his car.

As he pulled himself up into the driver's seat of the large SUV, Franklin considered his chances should he just pull away. Even if Brandt didn't manage to shoot him through the glass, there was nothing to stop him blowing out the wide tyres and chasing him down on foot. With a resigned intake of breath, he put the automatic gearbox in drive and allowed it to creep forward before selecting reverse. Listening to the familiar sound of the gravel pinging away from under the weight of the car, an instant later the back door opened, and Brandt slid himself quickly inside.

Despite the tinted windows he crouched down as Franklin pulled forward. 'Let him go in front.' His voice was a needless whisper. He waited until he heard the car go past before sitting up. Pulford was in an anonymous dark Ford Focus and was driving slowly to allow Franklin to catch up. 'Better follow him for a while,' he instructed as they settled into a steady gap behind. 'How far is the station?'

'About twenty minutes away.'

'Good, that gives us enough time.'

It took more than three miles for Brandt to feel confident that Pulford was no longer concerned about the extent of Franklin's intention to follow him all the way. He had gradually picked up speed and his desire to wait at junctions until there was a gap sufficient for the both of them had waned. 'Just a bit longer,' he muttered.

'Right, come off the gas a bit,' he said, observing the traffic lights on green at an intersection a couple of hundred metres up the road. 'Easy does it.' The gap between them had doubled by the time Pulford went through. 'Yesssss,' Brandt pumped his fist as they turned to amber less than a second later. With Franklin bringing the car to a halt, he stared ahead to see if Pulford's brake lights would come on. They did, but only a flicker, as he wiped off a touch of speed before taking the gentle bend head of him. 'Great, chuck a left here.'

'Want me to put the destination in the sat nav?' Franklin asked whilst making the manoeuvre, unable to hide the curiosity in his voice.

'No thanks, mate, I know exactly where we're going. Just keep following signs for the motorway.' The cheerfulness in his tone wasn't in the slightest bit forced.

Not only had he thought his way out of the sticky situation, but he now had it confirmed to him that the police were still a couple of steps behind. He was once again in a vehicle that wasn't linked to him, and this time he had no concerns that it might break down. He wriggled his backside to find the most comfortable position in the car's spacious rear seats and settled down for the long journey ahead.

His thoughts turned to DCI Johnson and how she was getting on.

Chapter Seven

There was no cruel, tantalising dream this time. One moment Johnson was unconscious and the next she was awake. However, it still took a few more seconds for her brain to explain the tremendous sense of loss she felt. McNeil was dead. Perhaps she had known it from the very moment his eyes had stopped seeing her and his hand went limp. He was dead because of her. She didn't know how that man, the man whose actions had first brought her and McNeil together and then conspired to keep them apart, knew where she lived. But of one thing she was certain. If it hadn't been for her, then McNeil would still be alive; she would most likely be dead but at least he would be safe somewhere.

The conflicting emotions swirling around Johnson's mind were threatening to cause her to scream again and she just managed to stop herself, for fear that she might be pinned to the bed once more and put back to sleep. It was only as she tried to put her right hand to her mouth to keep herself silent that she realised she had been strapped down. The sensation of only being able to waggle her limbs mere millimetres was too reminiscent of her attack to endure, and she let out a long, loud bellow of distress.

'Help, we need a nurse in here!'

The shout made Johnson look to the door. It was an officer but, thankfully, different to the one who had restrained her before. She opened her mouth to speak to him but, before she could, he moved out of the way to allow one of the medical staff to enter. Even if Johnson hadn't recognised her face, the nervous expression with which she regarded her would have been enough to confirm she was the nurse who had sedated her.

Her hesitation to approach gave Johnson enough time to speak. 'Please, please don't put me under again.' She had done her best to replace the hatred she felt towards this woman with a tone of fear.

'I... I...' was all she could manage to stutter, her eyes glancing towards the small bag of liquid attached to the IV drip.

'He tied me up like this.' Although her statement was met with confusion, it had served to make the nurse look at her again. 'The man who attacked me,' she added. There was no need to feign hurt this time. Bubbling under all the rage, the guilt and the bitterness Johnson felt, was the knowledge that she had been violated by this man. He may not have got as far as penetrating her, but he had stripped her, tied her up and even sunk his teeth into her body. She fought to push this aside knowing she would have to deal with it eventually but, for now, she needed to concentrate on finding out what had happened since then.

'Oh my god, I'm so sorry,' the woman cried, her face transformed. 'Here! Help me get her out of these.' She gestured for the man to attend to the other side of the bed. Despite her concern, no sooner had Johnson been freed from her shackles, she took three quick steps backwards to get herself out of arm's reach.

Johnson couldn't bring herself to thank the nurse and, instead, turned her attention to the officer. 'I need to speak to Potter.'

'I'm sorry?' He looked genuinely confused.

'Potter. I need to speak to Detective Superintendent Steven Potter.'

'But I… er…'

'Do you know who I am?'

'Er, no, miss. I wasn't told anything. I was told to come down and guard you. I was told that you weren't dangerous but then Blakey, I mean PC Blake, the officer I relieved, said you had gone mad and they had needed to, er… you know…' he said, pointing at the straps.

Despite her urgency to speak and find out what the hell was going on, she couldn't help but sigh. This was just typical, and the piss poor communication was something she had struggled with when she had first joined the force. As a new recruit, she had been frustrated at being given orders without any context, much less an explanation why. It wasn't that she was over-inquisitive; she believed that she would be able to do a better job if she understood all the facts.

'I'm DCI Stella Johnson,' she said simply. She could see his expression change as the name caused a spark of recognition, before he stared intensely past the hospital gown, and the bruising on her face that, no doubt, was replicated across much of her body following her impact with the road.

'Shit, sorry, ma'am,' he responded, unconsciously rubbing his head with embarrassment, not only for not realising who she was, but also for swearing in front of a superior. The slight bow he then gave, which was hastily repeated by the nurse, would have, under different circumstances, been amusing.

'Not your fault, but I do still need to talk to the DSI.'

'Erm, okay. Right. I'll call it in,' he said, lifting the radio attached to the front of his uniform. 'Nurse, do you have a mobile phone?' She started patting her pockets and now it was his turn to sigh. 'No, I mean one of those telephones on a trolley.'

'Sure,' she replied, running out of the room blushing.

It only took a couple of minutes to sort, but it seemed like an age for Johnson. The thought of the killer getting away was too much to bear but the longer she waited the more convinced she became that it was going to be bad news.

'Stella, how are you?' Potter must have been informed that she was trying to get hold of him. There was a desperation in his voice that seemed beyond just concern for her wellbeing.

'Have you got him?' She ignored his enquiry.

'Erm… well…'

'Fucking hell,' she wailed, resisting the temptation to throw the handset across the room. Her outburst was enough to cause the officer, who had remained on the inside of the door, to wince, and the nurse, who had been pretending to organise some items on the bedside table, to recoil.

'No, Stella, listen to me!' The power in his command silenced Johnson. 'We know who he is…'

'…he's the man from the CCTV.'

'Yes, yes we know that. We were able to get a clearer image of him, having traced the car back to the station.'

'What?'

'Just listen,' he repeated. 'We've been able to positively ID him.'

'Who is he?' She couldn't help herself interrupting once more.

'He's one of our own, Stella.' Potter's voice dropped. 'I… I recognised him. I'm so sorry, I should have seen it before, but the image was so grainy, and he was wearing a hat and…'

'Have you got him?' Her tone was cold, deadly.

'A team's just been dispatched now,' he said, brighter. 'ETA is…' A slight pause. 'Three minutes. Look, I'm overseeing this and need to…'

'You call me as soon as you've got him.' She slammed down the phone without waiting for a reply and turned to the nurse. 'How do I get this fucking thing out of my hand?' Johnson was already pulling at the cannula.

Chapter Eight

'Why can't we just pull into the services?'

'Don't be so fucking stupid!' Brandt had grown increasingly irritable during the long journey down to Folkestone. Tiredness had caught up with him and the paracetamol he had picked up from home was doing little to dull the throbbing in his head. Discovering that the Eurotunnel didn't run 24 hours a day and that it would be 6am until the first train had initially worried him. The getaway had been relatively clean, but he wouldn't be satisfied until they had made it across to the continent. He knew that if that nosey twat Pulford or someone else became sufficiently suspicious of Franklin's behaviour and decided to track his car's movements, they would know exactly where he was going. But he wasn't going to make it easy for them by spending the next few hours sitting under a load of CCTV cameras that would lead them directly to him. 'Pull off at the next junction.'

'Where are we going?'

'Stop asking me that and just do as I tell you!' Once the initial shock of events that evening had worn off, Franklin had become increasingly talkative. It seemed that whatever sleep he had managed after knocking off work early had done him good and he didn't seem to be succumbing to the same fatigue as Brandt. He had let him chat away, if for no other reason than it seemed to be doing a better job of preventing him inadvertently nodding off than the car's stereo.

Not that Franklin's chatter was a whole lot more interesting. Having established very early on that attempts to discover their ultimate destination and what would happen when they got there were unwelcome, he started talking about his wife and kids. Brandt knew exactly what he was up to; trying to personalise things was an obvious tactic for any abductee in the hope it would make it harder for the abductor to do them harm. Not only was it not working, but the more Brandt heard about how wonderful his wife was, notwithstanding their recent issues, and how bright and promising his children were, the more he detested Franklin. Even if only part of what he had been saying was true, it enraged him to think that someone as pathetic as him could end up with a better life than he had. Furthermore, he reasoned that freeing these people from such a dead weight might be doing them a favour.

'Take that single-track road on the right and I'll find us somewhere we can stop.'

'You're not… you're not going to…'

'Oh man up, Brian, I just need us to find somewhere quiet, so we can get forty winks before catching the train.' Even with just the dull illumination from the instrument panel Brandt could see that Franklin remained far from convinced that he wasn't going to shoot him and leave him in a ditch. 'Besides I had to make the booking using this car's registration, so it would be a bit odd if the owner didn't check-in at the terminal.' The logic to that statement elicited a small nod of acceptance.

'Look over there, you can stop in that entrance to the field.'

Franklin slowed the vehicle and pulled in, the car bouncing over the mud ruts left by the farmer's tractor.

'Ah, peace at last.' Brandt sighed, reaching for the rope he'd got out of his shed before they left. 'Right, I'm going to have to tie your hands or something, but feel free to recline your seat a bit if you want to first.'

Franklin stayed in the position he was and didn't move as Brandt clambered through to the front and secured him by looping the rope through the spokes of the steering wheel. He had just settled in the back again and was arranging his bag to act as a pillow when Franklin finally piped up again. 'Why did you do it?'

Brandt sighed. 'Why do you think? You don't think I know that the moment I drop off, you would be out that door and…'

'No,' he interrupted firmly. 'I mean, why did you kill all those people?'

'You wouldn't understand,' Brandt replied dismissively, closing his eyes.

The unexpected laughter that followed resulted in them immediately reopening. 'For fuck's sake, Jeff, you think I haven't met dozens of people like you in my whole career? Murderers!' There was much distaste in this last word, like it was an insect that had crawled into his mouth and needed to be ejected as quickly as possible.

Brandt sat up in a fit of rage and jabbed the Glock into his ribs. 'Don't you fucking dare compare me with those sick cunts.'

Silence.

He flicked off the safety and jammed the gun further into Franklin's side, awaiting the pathetic, begging apology that he was sure would follow.

It didn't.

'So how are you different?' Franklin asked calmly.

'Alright, I'll tell you!' Brandt hissed. 'The one thing they all have in common, which I don't have, is a need to kill. It might be for different reasons, but the need is the same. It might be because something in their childhood turned them into a sick fucking bastard or to give themselves a sense of power and worth that was missing in their pathetic little lives. Or they might simply do it because they can, and they get off on it! But I'm different, I'm not doing it for me.'

'Who are you doing it for?' Franklin had made no attempt to hide his incredulity, twisting round to stare directly into Brandt's eyes.

'For the same reason why all your tragic attempts to brown-nose and piggyback your way to the top hasn't worked. No one cares anymore. No one gives a shit about what we do. No one gives a flying fuck about a few fatal stabbings here and there as long as they have somewhere to go to get their next skinny latte and their broadband speed is reliable. People bang on about global terrorism and Brexit and all that shit but only because they think it might affect them. As long as the murderers keep killing their own wives and children, people get shot in a drug deal that went wrong, and women get raped whilst stumbling home from some seedy nightclub at 4am in the morning, they don't care. They don't care because it won't happen to them. It won't happen to them because their husband is an accountant at a respected multinational company, they don't do drugs or if they do, they don't have to go on the streets to get them, and if they do go out at night rather than get Deliveroo to bring them their favourite restaurant food, they book their Uber to arrive before they have even got up from the table.'

'What about those people who don't have a middle-class job or can't afford taxis to take them door to door?'

'They're too fucking thick to notice. If it isn't in the shitty rag of a newspaper they read, then they don't know it's even happening. And because the people that matter don't care, the newspapers don't bother to write about it.' Brandt was shouting by now, spittle flying from his mouth. 'And when someone lets these ignorant cunts have a say in what happens, we end up with Brexit, we end up with

Trump, and the world becomes an even shittier place than it was before.'

'Okay, okay,' Franklin said, the need to calm Brandt down was urgent, but the tirade had failed to answer one simple question. 'Tell me how you have made a difference then.'

'I don't really have to tell you, I could see it on your face when you went into that press conference.'

'What the…?'

'Come on, Brian, let's not dick around. You were going into the press conference to share with the public that one of their citizens, your citizens, had just been murdered in cold blood. You could barely keep the smile off your face.'

'How fucking dare you, Jeff! Don't tar me with your own brush.'

'Hold on, hold on, I'm not judging you, you're just a product of the society in which we live. You were delighted to be there. The media circus had finally come to town. Look, I don't blame you and, more than that, I understand. You've worked your whole life in law enforcement and how many times have you seen yourself on the news? I'm not talking about the shitty local stuff, I mean the proper news, the one people actually watch? All those crimes, all those criminals caught and barely a ripple made.'

'So, what, you did it for fame? Infamy?'

'No, no,' Brandt laughed. 'It's not about me. What I have done is stop people being complacent. By doing what I did anywhere and to anyone means that the wife of the accountant in her nice detached house, much like yours by the way, can no longer pass things off as affecting other people. She no longer feels safe when she nips to the shops.'

'But, Jeff, isn't the whole point of our job to make people feel safe?'

'No, it's not, and that's the problem. We're meant to make people be safe. Big fucking difference, Brian! The safety she used to feel was an illusion; a fallacy. And we can't make people be safe until they accept the danger that is all around them. Tell me, Brian, how many people have you charged, certain that they were guilty to only find them acquitted in the courts?'

'A few,' Franklin conceded meekly.

'More than a few I bet. Doesn't it bother you? And I tell you why it happens: because society lets it happen. It's so oblivious to what's really going on out there that it doesn't care whether murderers get off scot free.'

'Ah now come on, Jeff…'

'No, it's true. If people really wanted to clean up society, they would give up all this innocent-until-proven-guilty bullshit and they would put their trust back in us that we know what we're doing.'

'What are you going on about, Jeff? Are you actually being serious here? When people find out that it's a copper that's done all this, and not just any old copper but a fucking Detective Superintendent, what do you think that's going to do for trust in the police? I'll tell you what'll happen, it'll make what the Catholic Church suffered as a result of the child molesting priests look like a fucking picnic.'

Brandt shrugged. 'Can't make an omelette without breaking eggs and all that. Don't tell me that you don't know lots of coppers whom the force would be better off without. Take that Johnson bitch for example…'

'Why her?'

'Come on, I saw the look you gave her when she answered that question after you'd made it perfectly clear that you wouldn't be taking any. What's more, I bet you told her before you went in that she was to keep her pretty mouth shut. Didn't want her treading on your toes.'

'I don't see how her breaking protocol makes her a rotten apple.'

'She knew exactly what she was doing.' Brandt sneered. 'She wanted the press to run a story suggesting I was... I was... confused.'

'Is that why you picked girls then? Well, apart from that Asian guy on my patch. Was that to prove something to yourself?'

'What the fuck? Do you realise who you're talking to?' Brandt waved the gun in Franklin's face, outraged. He had entertained this prick's impertinent questions and had explained quite clearly that none of this was about him. Of all people, given that he must have gone through the same shit Brandt had in his career, he should have understood.

'Oh, I know exactly who I'm talking to. You say you're different to all the other murderers but you're the same as them, Jeff; exactly the fucking same. Your wife left you and you're too proud to wank off to the internet like the rest of us, so you get your sick kicks in another way. What's more...'

The sound of the back-door opening stopped Franklin. Moments later Brandt was next to him, trying to yank him out and into the dirt, forgetting that his hands were still attached to the steering wheel. As Brandt let go of his feet Franklin slumped awkwardly on the door sill, his arms held aloft. 'Please don't,' he cried, closing his eyes and turning his face in anticipation of the flurry of punches that would surely follow.

It was with surprise that he could feel himself being untied.

'Get up,' Brandt ordered.

Franklin did as he was told, all the while staring through the darkness at the gun in front of him. He wondered whether his brain would process his eyes viewing the muzzle flash before he felt the impact of the bullet.

He wasn't yet ready to accept his fate, not until he knew that Brandt wouldn't go after his family next.

'But you need me to… in order to get to France. You said so…'

Brandt paused, debating whether to shoot this prick there and then. As he applied pressure to the trigger, he knew that it would require an alteration to his plans but not in the way Franklin anticipated. Did he think he was fucking stupid? Did he think they were just going to rock up to the terminal; the two of them, all smiles, whilst they both handed over their passports to the border guard? But after a day of unwanted improvisation Brandt wasn't going to be responsible for yet another deviation from a cast iron plan. He nodded to himself.

'Get in the boot,' he said coldly.

'What?'

'Now!' Brandt roared, grabbing Franklin by the collar and dragging him round to the back of the car. He released him, so he could open the tailgate whilst keeping the gun trained on him.

'But… but you need me… you bought two tickets…'

'Who said I bought two tickets?' Brandt laughed, bundling him into the boot and stuffing a handkerchief in his mouth. 'Spit it out and I'll rip out your tongue.' He then turned Franklin over, tying his hands behind him before flipping him back again. All that remained was to secure the gag with a smaller bit of rope from his shed.

'There,' he said, patting his hands theatrically. 'All done. And before you say it – well, if you could say it – don't even think about making a load of noise when we get to Folkestone.' To emphasise the point, he pulled out of his pocket the scrunched-up bit of paper with Franklin's family's address. He took one final look at his wild, panicked eyed and slammed the tailgate shut.

Climbing into the back again and resting his head on the makeshift pillow, Brandt felt a lot calmer. He didn't know why he hadn't thought of doing this as soon as they pulled up. At least this way he could get a couple of hours' sleep without worrying whether Franklin would find some means of escape.

But sleep didn't come. Despite his exhaustion, the anxiety of the border crossing weighed heavily on his mind and he sat there thinking as the light of dawn gradually arrived. At least his concerns of what was to come provided some distraction from thoughts of earlier. Some of Franklin's stinging words had rung true. It had never been Brandt's intention for people to find out it was an ex-policeman who was doing these things. Moreover, he had hoped to build on his successes and take advantage of the momentum his exploits had gained. Undoubtedly his visit to Johnson's house would be headline news, but he had wanted the spotlight to continue to fall on his victims, whilst his identity would remain a mystery. He took some comfort from the knowledge that they had been closer to catching him than he'd thought. In actual fact, his impetuousness in targeting Johnson rather than another random person may well have saved him. He would be sat at home now, congratulating himself on another job well done, unaware that the police had plucked his face from the hundreds of others around the various crime scenes. Maybe Franklin would still have foolishly come to see him, but he doubted that, had he not enticed him to the football the day before to ply him with enough drink so that he gave away a crucial detail about Johnson, things would have turned out that way.

But he wasn't safe yet. With that knowledge firmly rooted in his mind Brandt started up the car at exactly 5am. It would give him an hour to make the short final drive to the Eurotunnel and board his train.

*　*　*

The clock on the X5's dashboard told him it was 5:13am as he took the exit from the motorway; the terminal visible a little further up the slip road. He hadn't heard a peep from his companion, even though starting the engine must have given Franklin a fright.

It was Franklin's much more expensive overnight bag that he'd selected to be sat next to him as he made his approach. Not only did he want his cheap item out of sight, but he also would be using Franklin's passport, not least in case the police had managed to identify him in the meantime. Brandt knew this was the weakest part of his plan but his study of the photograph back at the house had confirmed, especially considering it had been taken a few years ago, that they had more than a passing resemblance. It didn't stop him feeling nervous, but he hoped that whoever he met would be sufficiently demotivated at this time of day not to notice the subtle differences.

Brandt's relief that the first barrier was automated didn't last when he found he could no longer recall the entirety of the car's registration number. He started hunting round for Franklin's phone which he had reactivated to make the reservation online, but a quick glance at the machine showed him that the plate had been recognised and matched with his booking.

With the barrier now waiting patiently in its vertical position, he moved forward the couple of hundred yards to border control. He neither wanted to look reluctant nor too keen, but kept the window wound down from before; the rush of the cool morning air a welcome refresh to his senses.

'Hallo,' said the young woman in a thick French accent, who sat in the kiosk level with Brandt. 'Passport and ticket please.'

'Er sure,' he replied, pretending to search in his bag. 'Here you go,' he said cheerfully a few moments later. It wasn't like immigration in some countries he had visited where he was asked the reasons for his visit. As she flipped to the relevant page and quickly compared his name to the one on the ticket before handing it back to him, he wondered whether things would be different once Britain left the EU. Pleased by the relative lack of attention, he placed the items back in his bag and reached for the gear selector in anticipation of being waved on.

'Can you open the windows please.'

'Excuse me?'

'The windows… the ones at the back. I need to see past the privacy glass.'

'Oh, I see!' Brandt cried, a little too loudly, fumbling for the relevant switch. He had deactivated the car's stop/start system hoping the diesel engine's clatter would cover up any noises from the boot, but he was sure Franklin would have heard him responding to the request. In a similar situation, Brandt was sure he would take the opportunity to signal for help but, with the French woman now satisfied, he was able to sigh a breath of relief and creep onto the customs area unimpeded.

The layout was such that particular cars could be siphoned off from the queuing traffic to be searched in a number of covered bays, but the whole area seemed lifeless except for the man in the cabin at the end, who raised the barrier even before Brandt approached. It would seem that smugglers and terrorists weren't perceived as keen on the early start afforded by the first train of the day.

The road led around to a large parking area with a building similar to a motorway services; signs outside advertising some of the concessions within. He regarded the Starbucks logo with regret at not being in a position to go in and buy himself a large cup of black coffee. His full bladder was conspiring to try and convince him it would be a good idea to stretch his legs, but ignoring both it and the caffeine receptors in his brain, he pulled up in front of one of the large information boards instead. He would wait to urinate until he was on the train and, as he gazed up at the screen informing him that boarding would be called soon, he wondered whether Franklin had pissed himself yet.

'Just one last stage,' he exhaled to himself.

As smooth as things had gone, he knew that until he cleared the terminal at the other side, he wasn't safe. Then again, he was no longer Jeffrey Brandt and if they started looking for Brian Franklin then they would be able to trace the car throughout France's motorway network. But there was little point worrying about that now, and he waited patiently until all the vehicles were loaded and the internal metal doors swung in to close off the different compartments. With the man in the van behind apparently content to spend the journey in his seat, Brandt pulled on a flat cap he found in the back of the car and followed the signs to the grotty toilet whilst the speaker informed him of the emergency procedures first in English and then French.

Having arrived back to find no one crowded round his tailgate listening to the muffled cries for help within, Brandt settled back in the car and, with the train finally departing, he began drifting off to sleep.

He was jolted awake less than half an hour later by the sounds of engines being switched on. Not only had he missed the entire journey, but he also had failed to notice when they had stopped and the sound of the internal doors retracting. The car in front had already moved off before Brandt remembered where he had put the key and, with the delay appropriately large for the van driver behind to give an impatient blip of his horn, he yanked the selector into Drive and sped off, determined to close the gap with the car in front to an acceptable distance before they disembarked.

Sunshine greeted Brandt and he opened the window to take in his first gulp of cool French air. The line of vehicles continued steadily on and, before he realised it, they were fed onto the motorway. He had never driven on the continent before, but it didn't take long for him to get used to the, initially alien, feeling of driving on the wrong side of the road.

After a few kilometres of careful driving and with the, now programmed, sat nav telling him he had hundreds more until he reached his destination, he worked out how to use the X5's cruise control and relaxed into the steady 120kph trip across Northern France. Brandt didn't speak any French, but he remembered part of a song his sister used to sing when they were kids. His rendition of *Alouette, Gentille Alouette*, fifty years on, bore little resemblance but he repeated the same few lines over and over again, increasing the volume each time in the hope that Franklin would be able hear his jovial voice in the confines of the boot.

Chapter Nine

DSI Potter didn't call Johnson back as requested. He drove to the Queen's Medical Centre instead. He had needed to go and see her anyway, both as a colleague and a friend, but it was a little awkward leaving so soon after the police operation. Not that there was anything he could do specifically for now. Brandt's house had been empty and with no sign of anything untoward. Perhaps examination of the contents of his computer's hard drive would reveal something but, if it wasn't Potter himself who recognised him in the images from outside the police station yesterday afternoon, he would be starting to wonder whether a mistake had been made.

Even though the sting had been in the early hours of the morning, the commotion had been enough to wake some of the neighbours. They would all be spoken to in due course, but those who had emerged once the area was declared secure didn't have much to say about Brandt, except that he tended to keep to himself and he had been alone since his wife left a few years before. No one was able to confirm whether Brandt had been at home that evening; the person living opposite thought she heard a car pull up at some point, but she couldn't be sure it was at

Brandt's house and hadn't thought to look out of her window. ANPRs showed he had travelled in that direction, but the hits stopped beyond his house. They hadn't retrieved the vehicle yet, but Potter was sure he must have dumped it somewhere. It made no sense to him that Brandt would go to the effort of using a different car, one that was currently registered to a man in Yorkshire and not on the stolen vehicle database, only to drive it straight back home again afterwards.

That there was nothing more that could realistically be done at this point wasn't a comfort to Potter as he parked up and considered how he was going to explain this to Johnson. The truth was he felt he had let her down. He hadn't approved of her unorthodox taunting of Brandt in the press, but he should not have let himself get caught up in other matters; those relating to the carpet fibre found on the body of the man in Milton Keynes. He should have realised that she had placed herself in personal danger and taken steps to protect her. Moreover, he was frustrated with himself for not recognising Brandt in the still she had pulled from the earlier CCTV footage. Now he knew it was Brandt in that grainy photograph, it seemed all too obvious.

The coward in Potter hoped he would find Johnson asleep and he would ask the nurse to tell her he had visited when she woke. However, he very much doubted that would be the case. He had worked with Stella Johnson for many years and was well aware of her tenacity. When she hadn't heard from him within a few minutes of their earlier call she would have been haranguing the officer on guard to find out the details. He just hoped that she had been unsuccessful because, much as Potter dreaded what awaited, he knew it would be better coming from him.

The receptionist at A & E informed him that she had been transferred to one of the wards and, as he made his way along the maze of corridors, his mind turned back to Brandt; specifically, where he was and what he was doing.

If he was as much of a loner as he had been led to believe, then he wondered where he had managed to hole up. And it wasn't as though this was a storm in a teacup that would blow over in a few days. By mid-morning his face would be plastered over all the major news networks and someone, somewhere would recognise him even if he hadn't left a trail from where he dumped the car. There was no chance of him fleeing the country because his details had been sent to every port and airport in the British Isles. Believing it to be just a matter of time until Brandt was apprehended, he felt a little better as he pushed through the final set of double doors.

Potter didn't need to go to the efforts of visiting the desk to find out which room Johnson was in, the commotion that greeted him on the ward confirmed her whereabouts.

'Give me some fucking clothes!' She was berating one of the nurses whilst the uniformed officer was attempting to squeeze himself between them.

'I've told you already, we don't have any. Please just go back inside your room and we can…'

'Fine then!' But Johnson did not turn towards the open door; instead she started marching down the corridor. 'I'll just have to go like this,' she shouted over her shoulder, the hospital gown flapping in her wake.

Johnson stopped when she saw who was standing just inside the ward. 'Guv?'

'Is there somewhere we can talk?' he called past her.

'Er…' the nurse replied nervously, wondering whether it would be a bad idea to say they could use Johnson's room. 'Er, yes… there's a family area just down there,' she finally said, pointing to a corridor on the left.

Given Johnson's barely concealed nakedness, Potter decided to break with his usual impersonal body language; wrapping his arm round her and leading her inside the place the nurse had indicated. He could see from the way it was laid out, the posters on the pin board publicising various counselling services, this was where bad news was delivered to patients' loved ones. He eschewed the chair he guessed the doctor used, electing instead to sit Johnson on the sofa, where he sat next to her.

'You didn't call me,' she stated blandly, pulling her legs under her and wrapping the gown protectively around herself.

'I wanted to discuss face to face. How are you? I understand the X-rays show there are no broken bones.'

'Where is he?'

'He wasn't there but he can't have gone far. We've tracked the vehicle he used and are...' Potter stopped. He could see from the expression on Johnson's face that she knew exactly what procedures were going to be followed now and that none of them was a source of comfort.

'He killed him.'

'I know,' he said simply. 'I'm so sorry, I know the two of you had grown... close.'

Johnson's eyes started welling up. 'I don't know what he was doing there.' Potter could feel the unfamiliar prick of his own tears forming. 'He saved me,' she added in barely more than a whisper.

'You don't need to talk about this now,' he said, as much for his benefit as hers.

'I need to go and see him.'

'I'm not sure it's a good idea...' he responded, weakly.

'Please, guv,' her eyes were imploring. 'I... I went to get help and I was going to go back to him... but he had gone out the door and I chased him... and I... I...' Sobs prevented her saying anymore.

Potter embraced Johnson in an effort to console her. He waited, clutching her tightly whilst her body heaved in anguish, his own tears falling silently down his cheeks.

Chapter Ten

Johnson had seen many dead bodies over the years, but this was the first one she had known personally since her mother had died whilst she was still a teenager. She was treated differently as well; not there in a professional capacity, the mortuary assistant was keen to keep the viewing as short as possible. This was fine by Johnson. With no facial injuries, his serene expression could nearly have convinced her he was merely asleep, were it not for the austere and clinical condition of the room. Much as she was frustrated with Potter for not having caught his killer, she was touched by the uncharacteristic show of warmth in the way he had held her whilst she gave in to her despair for a brief moment.

When she had made it clear that she would be leaving the hospital he had insisted that he drive her. Potter had asked about whether there were any friends or family she could stay with and she had hoped that her simple shake of her head would be enough. But he pressed the matter and she confessed that the photograph of her nephew on her desk was there more for appearance's sake, and that he was actually an adult now living abroad with her sister. There followed the inevitable offer from Potter that she stay at his house for a while. The easy way he accepted her refusal confirmed her suspicion that this was perhaps a step too far for his sense of appropriateness, but he had insisted on arranging a hotel, claiming she did not need to worry about its immediate cost. They were half way there when they both realised she was still in just her hospital gown and, having established that neither of them would feel particularly comfortable with him shopping for clothes for her, especially as it would need to include underwear, he detoured via her house.

Her whole street had been blocked off to prevent motorists having to double back once they saw the police cordon placed across the road to support the forensics investigation. Having navigated the barrier, Potter parked sufficiently away from the property to keep her view obscured. It was a sensible and sensitive move but ultimately futile because her mere presence there caused detailed memories of the attack to come flooding back, especially because she could see the damaged form of McNeil's car parked behind the sparkling red of her own.

Johnson studied the bandages on her right hand, which she had used to smash in Brandt's passenger window with the assistance of her neighbour's rockery. Not only was she amazed that she had managed to do so, but the fact she hadn't broken any bones seemed remarkable. The impact with the road was still a hazy memory, but she suspected the thudding in her head was from more than the punch that had knocked her out when she was first accosted.

Potter looked rather sheepish when he returned a few minutes later, which did cause a small smile to form on her lips. Sifting through her drawers to find her a few complete outfits, she hoped to God he'd had the good sense to avoid her bedside drawer. She knew he would be too ashamed to admit if he had gone in there but the thought of him withdrawing one of its items, turning it over in his hands whilst staring at it quizzically, caused a shiver to run down her spine.

'Er, I hope I got everything,' he said, passing her a tightly stuffed bag.

She turned and placed it on one of the back seats. 'I'm sure it will be fine,' she replied, trying to put as much warmth as she could into her voice; hiding the numbness she felt within.

'I even nipped into the bathroom to get you some make up.' He turned to her with a look of horror on his face. 'I didn't mean you need to put on any by the way. You look fine and, anyway, you…'

She placed a hand on his arm to stop him. 'Honestly, it's fine. Thank you for doing this, Steven.' Use of his forename was odd on her lips but seemed the best way of reassuring him.

They sat in silence for the short journey to the Crown Plaza, situated close to the city centre. Potter didn't like the idea of Johnson brooding but, believing small talk to be inappropriate given the circumstances, he didn't want to say anything about what had happened for fear of making things worse.

Relieved that there was nowhere to park at the front of the hotel, and with Potter only able to pull into a drop-off bay, she insisted he let her go rather than seek out a space in the multi-storey behind it.

'I'll be fine,' she said in response to the look he gave the hospital gown she was still wearing. 'I'll get changed in the ladies' before checking in. Don't think I don't appreciate this, but I need you to get back and find that bastard.' Whether it was the venom with which she uttered the last word or the fact that he had spent longer away from the station than he really should have under the circumstances, she didn't know, but as soon as he gave a small nod of acceptance, she opened the car door.

Johnson didn't look back as she carried her bag through the entrance to the Crown Plaza. Ignoring the looks of surprise she was sure her appearance was receiving, she focused on taking the most direct path to the toilets, indicated by a small glass sign attached to the ceiling.

A few minutes later, and dressed in a top and jeans that she would never normally wear in combination, she used the passkey she had been given at check-in to open up her room. It was clean and modern and with all the luxurious touches she would expect from a hotel of this reputation, but she was interested in none of these. She discarded her bag at the door; the blue of the hospital gown poking out between the zip. As she had stood naked in the toilet cubicle earlier, observing her battered and bruised body, the rush of emotion that had seen her break down in front of Potter threatened to return. Rather than allow herself to succumb within those unpleasant confines, she had hastily finished dressing and rushed to reception. Now that she was finally shut away in her own room she collapsed on the bed, unable to withhold her grief any longer.

Chapter Eleven

It did not take much time for the benefit of the short nap in the Eurotunnel to fade. Without the spikes of adrenaline helping to keep him alert, and the novelty of driving on the wrong side of the road wearing off, Brandt started to feel weary. The road through northern France was nowhere as busy as the British motorways. The landscape was dull. He desperately wanted to pull into a service station and get a few hours' sleep, but he would not let his successful escape from the country lull him into a false sense of security. In many respects he was grateful to DC Pulford for providing a stark indication that Franklin would be missed. Clearly his absence hadn't led to him being traced before they had made it to Folkestone, but that didn't mean they weren't near to doing so.

Brandt's decision to head east, rather than plunge south into France, had been a deliberate, albeit hastily conceived one. Knowing that the police would at least suspect he had accompanied Franklin, he wanted to mask his true destination by appearing to travel in a different direction. Once he had ditched Franklin and his vehicle, with the assumption being he was continuing on to either Germany or the Netherlands, it should buy him enough time to complete the rest of his journey unimpeded.

Crossing into Belgium after little more than an hour's driving gave Brandt the boost to his senses he required. Having used the car's sat nav to identify a suitable stopping point, he followed the E40's natural bend southeast in the direction of Brussels. The X5's fuel gauge was getting low, but the trip computer suggested that it had enough diesel to get them to their destination.

Half an hour later, they deviated from their course to Belgium's capital, turning left onto the E17 and swinging around the city of Ghent. Built in the Middle Ages as a port leading to the sea, it had grown much in the same way London had in its early years. The attractive stone buildings visible at its centre, dominated by the Castle of the Counts, were a welcome relief to the blandness of the journey so far. And yet it was the industrial areas that had since been built around it that brought Brandt the most comfort, because it was here he would shortly head, hoping to look like a migrant worker at one of the many factories and industrial plants.

Brandt knew he was in a positive frame of mind because, much as he disliked football, he found himself impressed by the sight of the Ghelamco Arena that passed on his right. It wasn't anywhere near as large as The Emirates which he had attended with Franklin just a couple of days before, but the developers had gone to a lot of effort to make this new stadium attractive with its front of mirrored glass. That he had never heard of the team K.A.A. Gent was of little concern as it gradually passed from view. He was nearing his turn off and started to consider the finer details of what was to follow.

Brandt had observed the odd set of traffic cameras throughout their route, but now off the main roads he was reassured that their progress could not be followed. He had selected the Doonkmeer lake, not just because of its location, but its size meant he should be able to find a secluded spot away from its early summer visitors. He carried on past the main car park which, despite being a weekday, contained a fair number of vehicles whose occupants had either stopped for a picnic or hired one of the various boats or water bikes. The road narrowed as he circumnavigated the lake and, with no further stop off points, he waited until the terrain was sufficiently flat for him to use the SUV's four-wheel drive capabilities to pull onto the grass. Brandt did not care about the branches of the low hanging trees pinging off the windscreen and scraping the paint on the sides of the car as he made his way to the water's edge, because the foliage would serve to obscure them from anyone driving past. The going was bumpy but there wasn't even a flicker of the X5's traction control's dashboard light; the recent weather having dried out the mud underneath.

With the engine switched off, Brandt allowed himself a few moments' peace before getting out of the car. What a 24 hours it had been and, this time yesterday, as he set off for Nottinghamshire police station, he would never have expected to find himself here. But despite all the drama of what had followed, sat there with the window open to allow the warm breeze to refresh his features and watching the calm water glinting in the sunlight, he felt reasonably satisfied. Much as it irked him that his plan to prove to DCI Johnson that her cruel claims of him being sexually confused were false had failed, it gave him comfort that he still remained at least one step ahead of the authorities. He had wanted to keep on killing until the British people had awoken from their slumber of indifference, but he knew he still had the opportunity to make his previous exploits have more of an impact if he could shock society by it not appearing the work of one man. If he could exert one final pressure on Franklin, he could make the controversy surrounding the involvement of an ex-policeman multiply exponentially.

'Okey dokey, here we go.' Brandt chuckled to himself, opening the door.

He laughed again as he opened the boot to observe Franklin cower away both from him and the blinding light. The smell of piss and shit hit him before he even noticed the dark stain on his trousers. Glancing around to check they remained unobserved, he hoisted Franklin up before allowing him to collapse on the ground outside.

'Brian, I'm going to untie you now,' he said slowly and deliberately as though talking to a child. 'Don't forget that I still have a gun in case you think about trying to make a run for it.' He started with the gag first, keen to gauge Franklin's reaction. When nothing was said he continued to cut the bonds securing his hands. Although he had tied them loosely he could see the abrasions from where he must have struggled in an attempt to free himself. 'You can get up now,' he said, helping him gain his feet.

'Where... where are we?' Franklin asked, still blinking against the rays from the sun.

'Do you like it? I said that we were going on holiday, didn't I?'

'What now?' He stared directly at Brandt despite the fear that was evident in his features.

'I think we had better sit down,' he replied, enjoying the look of recognition these words brought, so typically a precursor to bad news. Brandt hadn't planned any of this conversation but was enjoying the impact of his improvisation. He led him to the driver's seat and closed the door after him. Rather than keep the gun trained on him as he rounded the bonnet to the passenger side, he waved the key instead in a mocking gesture that demonstrated his inability to escape.

Sitting down with an audible sigh, Brandt turned to face him. 'Would you mind opening all the windows, I think we could do with a little more ventilation considering you have... well, you know... I then want you to put your hands on the wheel and keep them there until I tell you differently.' Franklin did as he was told, all the while staring forwards. Brandt once again saw the marks on his wrists but shrugged knowing there was nothing he could do about them now, hoping that with a little time and water they should fade.

'Well, let's cut to the chase, Brian. You're going to die now but not before you get the chance to say goodbye.'

Franklin's head snapped across to face him, but whether his look of surprise came from the revelation that he was about to be killed or the confusing statement that followed, Brandt couldn't tell. Instead, he gave him a look that he hoped seemed kind and gently nodded his head. 'Yes, I'm afraid so, but I want you to know that I wish it could have worked out differently. You've been a good friend,' he lied.

'If you just let me go...' Franklin pleaded. 'I'll tell them... I'll tell them...'

'Tell them what?' Brandt asked patiently. When Franklin was unable to reply he continued: 'You see that's the point. Believe me, if I could think of some way of this panning out differently, I would, but this is the only way.'

'They'll still catch you,' he said flatly, a look of resignation now etched on his face.

'Well you're going to help me with that. You're going to write a farewell note and I am going to dictate its contents.'

'Why the fuck would I do that?!' Franklin spat, a little bit of defiance emerging to dilute some of the despair.

'Well, a number of reasons,' Brandt replied evenly. 'The first I suppose is what does it matter to you given you'll be dead and all. I don't know whether you are a religious man, Brian, but either way it works out the same. If you do believe in an afterlife, then God or whoever will know the truth and still admit you through the pearly gates. If you're an atheist like me then what does it matter how people think you died, you'll just be... well, er, dead.'

Franklin opened his mouth to respond but a raised finger shushed him. 'That was just the first reason. The second is a bit more straightforward. As I said you're about to die; I'm sorry but there really is no movement on that, I'm afraid. You may probably have guessed but I want it to look like suicide. Now here's the thing about suicide: people tend to want to go in the most painless way possible. And I want that for you, Brian, I really do, but if you won't play ball and refuse to make it seem like you've taken your own life, then I'll be forced to make it more… well, how shall I put it – difficult.'

Again, the mouth opened and again Brandt signalled that he didn't want to be interrupted. 'Look, let me save you the details but, suffice to say, it would be slow and painful.' He paused to allow Franklin's imagination to consider what he might do. 'But before you make your decision, there is one last thing. I hate to bring it up, truly, but there is also the matter of your family.' Brandt couldn't stifle the smile that greeted Franklin's look of horror. 'I understand that you may be thinking they're safe now, what with us being in another country and everything, but there is something you should consider. If you're right with what you said before about the police catching me, and you won't allow me the opportunity to make a clean getaway, then what's to stop me going out in a blaze of glory starting with your wife and kids? Bit of a hassle getting all the way back there but, then again, who would be looking out for me re-entering the country?'

A few minutes later Franklin was shaking his head. He had only written the opening line to his suicide note but had stopped when Brandt dictated the next sentence. 'I can't…'

'I get it, Brian, I really do,' Brandt said, trying to sound calm and patient despite how he was feeling. The truth was, much that he hadn't expected it to be easy, he was anxious to be done and away. More than anything, he'd had enough of this pathetic wretch and, although he

76

wouldn't have the satisfaction of pulling the trigger himself, he wanted to see him dead. 'It must be hard for you balancing your hard-earned reputation against the safety of your family, knowing that whatever fond memories they have of you will be tarnished by what you must write. Perhaps it would be better for them to die instead, in the belief that you remained a good, decent man.'

'No,' he responded, simply but firmly, the pen touching the paper once more. And, even though there was worse to follow, he didn't hesitate until he had finished writing everything he was told.

'Good chap and, if it's any consolation to you, should I be caught, I'll be sure to tell everyone the truth,' Brandt said, injecting false sincerity into his voice, and slipping the note inside the clear plastic cover of the car's instruction manual. Closing it back inside the glovebox he took a deep breath. 'Now here's how we're going to do this: I'm going to move into the back seat directly behind you. In my right hand I will be holding a knife to your throat and, with my left, I am going to pass you the gun. You're going to hold it under your chin like this.' Brandt showed Franklin exactly where he wanted him to place the muzzle. 'If I even sense that you are thinking about doing anything else with the gun then I will cut your throat, dump you in the lake and head straight back to Calais. Clear?'

'Fucking coward!'

Rather than Brandt give credit to Franklin for not even hesitating to pull the trigger once he had finished his countdown a couple of minutes later, he was repulsed by his lack of fight. Brandt didn't have any children, but he was sure that if someone threatened to kill his wife if he didn't feign his own suicide, he would only be too pleased to sacrifice the bitch.

With a sigh he got out of the back of the car and approached the lake to wash his arms, having had the foresight to roll up his sleeves before he reached round to

Franklin. The gun shot had been alarmingly loud, causing birds in nearby trees to take flight. Brandt had made some makeshift ear plugs in anticipation of the explosion in the confined space of the X5, but he didn't think anyone who heard it on the faraway shore would believe it anything more than a farmer clearing his field of vermin.

Relieved that he would be pulling on his gloves for one final time, he went back to the X5 and opened the driver's door. He only glanced at the mess of Franklin's head as he reached across him to insert the key. Brandt was initially perplexed by his subsequent prod of the starter button failing to ignite the engine, but then remembered that it would only fire when the brake pedal was depressed. Although he managed to move Franklin's leg into the correct position, he couldn't get it to apply enough pressure, so, whilst mumbling a string of expletives under his breath, he kicked it away and pressed down with his own. With the starter button now able to do its job, he moved the gear selector into drive and released the electric handbrake. The car crept forward under its own torque and Brandt moved himself out of the way to watch it crawl slowly towards the lake. The angle of the bank was shallow, but its steady progress soon had its front wheels submerged. As the bonnet went beneath the water Brandt heard the clatter of the diesel engine take on a different note as the air box struggled to provide it with the oxygen needed to spark the fuel. After a couple more feet there was a sucking noise as it drew water into the pistons and died. Fortunately, the level was high enough to flood the windows and the car continued to slide into the lake, with the added weight now conspiring to drag it down further.

Brandt cursed himself for not having opened the sunroof to allow the last of the air to escape, but he felt confident that the top of the car would only be visible to anyone who was close by and, being black, only if they were looking directly at it. Besides, Brandt wanted the vehicle along with its contents to be found, just not before he had managed to put as much distance between him and them as possible.

Satisfied that there was no more that could be done, he glanced at his watch and slung his bag over his shoulder. He wasn't sure how far it was to the outskirts of the city, but he was convinced that a steady pace should see him there long before nightfall.

Chapter Twelve

Johnson dreaded three things, so she decided to do them all on the same day. She started by entering her house for the first time since that fateful evening, having checked out of the hotel early due to now being thoroughly sick of the buffet breakfast. It had been the longest week of her life, with nothing to do except trying, and failing, to come to terms with what had happened. After a couple of days, and with her physical injuries having remarkably reduced to little more than aches and pains, she had phoned Potter with her intention to return to work. Despite his attempted assurances, Brandt had seemingly disappeared, and she wanted to get involved in the hunt. Potter had been reluctant to share anything with her and it was from another colleague that she heard about the mysterious link with DSI Franklin. His car had been tracked into Belgium but from there the trail had gone cold. His fleeing suggested he at least had knowledge of Brandt's crimes, and it transpired that they had even spent the whole day together before he attacked her in Nottingham. However, it also seemed they may have gone their separate ways, with Franklin trying to make it out of the country before his connection with Brandt was discovered.

But Potter had denied her request to come back to work, stating that she would need to pass both a physical and a psychological examination. He flatly refused to entertain the idea of this happening before McNeil was buried so Johnson, much to his consternation, had booked it for an hour after he would be laid to rest.

There was nothing in her street that gave a clue to the events that had taken place there. Her red Audi TTRS was still parked outside the house and McNeil's blue Ford Fiesta must have either been towed away or taken by a relative. If the funeral wasn't going to be bad enough, the idea of meeting his family made Johnson sick to her stomach. Much as she wanted one final opportunity to say goodbye to McNeil, she planned on maintaining as low a profile as possible. However, she knew there was little chance of being able to do so, especially with the papers using stills from the press conferences to plaster her all over their front covers. Fortunately, McNeil's image had remained outside of the public domain but there were bound to be reporters at the church.

She guessed the absence of anyone outside her house was in the belief that she wouldn't be allowed to return there whilst Brandt was on the loose. The fact of the matter was that she intended putting it on the market immediately and had already used some of the time she'd spent kicking her heels in the hotel finding herself a place to rent in the meantime. She had planned on taking her own car from here but decided it would be easier to just have the taxi wait, especially as she hadn't yet picked up a parking permit for her new flat. The driver seemed only too pleased to stay, safe in the knowledge that every minute Johnson spent inside would add to the overall fare. She rushed up to the front door, concerned that one of her neighbours might come out and try to talk to her. Observing the fresh paint where the repairs had been made, she pulled out the new keys the locksmith had delivered to her.

Johnson's first impression inside was that it no longer smelled like her house. She had never before given consideration to the team of people whose job it was to clean up crime scenes once the forensics had finished their work, but the chemicals used by them indicated a thorough job. The flooring literally sparkled in the morning sunshine and, had it not been for the marks on the wall where the blood had been scrubbed off, she could almost believe she had imagined the whole thing. The sitting room appeared to be as she had left it, save for the cushions on the sofa being arranged differently to normal, and the telephone had been placed back on its charger. She could see the crack on the plastic at the top of it, presumably the result of the impact following her hurling the device in an effort to get back to McNeil as quickly as possible.

Much as Potter had done an admirable job of collecting essentials for her stay at the hotel, she would need to brave returning to the scene of McNeil's death if she were going to find clothing appropriate for the funeral. She took the stairs slowly, remembering the sickening thud of McNeil falling down them. At the time she hadn't realised he had been fatally wounded in the process, with that only becoming apparent when he had somehow made it back up to her with Brandt's knife sticking out of his chest. His decision to sacrifice any chance of his own survival so that she could free herself, seemed all the more wrong as she observed her bedroom. Only the faded stain on the carpet where he had bled out indicated what had happened there. Her wrought iron bed, which she had been tied naked to, now appeared as normal, with just the bare mattress sitting on it, presumably with the sheet and duvet taken away for further forensic testing.

In many respects, she would have preferred the room to look as she had left it because at least it would reflect the tremendous grief inside her that had done nothing to abate in the past week. She took the symbolism of the sparse room as an unwelcome indication that she should now be looking to move on in the same way it had. But she would not, could not, do that. Not after the funeral and when she had been granted a return to work. Not even when Brandt was found. She would not allow the memory of what had happened to McNeil to become an unpleasant stain that she tried to remove. She needed to again look into the eyes of the man responsible, but this time knowing that he was now the person cuffed and with no future to speak of.

With the rage bubbling up inside her, she set to work finding a black suit and white shirt, forcing herself to also collect more clothes to last her until she had washed the items that Potter had retrieved for her and were currently bagged up in the boot of the taxi.

It was with defiance that she closed the front door, with the new mechanism making an unfamiliar latching sound. Abandoning thoughts of selling it, she could not allow herself to be driven from her home. As soon as Brandt was arrested, she would return there and every morning, as she regarded the carpet by her bed, she would be reminded of what had been denied her.

Johnson regretted releasing the taxi once it had taken her to her rented apartment, located in Nottingham's Trent Bridge area, ironically just a short walk from Sarah Donovan, Brandt's first victim, and close to his third which had taken place along the river itself. It wasn't so much that the new one arrived late, causing her to wait outside for over ten minutes, it was the look of recognition he gave her, rather than one of apology, that troubled Johnson. Having become increasingly irritated by the frequent glances he gave her in the rear-view mirror, she eventually demanded he come out and say it. However, rather than embarrass him into leaving her alone altogether, it only served to bring forth a barrage of questions that lasted the remainder of the journey. She wanted nothing more than to tell him to fuck off and mind his own business but, knowing his next call was likely to be to the local newspaper, she politely responded whilst attempting to say as little as possible. She didn't give a toss what the press had to say about her, but she knew that it would undermine her chances of a swift return to work if she was seen to be behaving irrationally.

Johnson's subterfuge of calm was forced to remain as they pulled up at the church. As expected, there were a number of journalists and the camera flashes commenced as soon as she got out, after reluctantly giving her driver a substantial tip. She had considered wearing dark glasses to complete the incognito look but didn't want to appear aloof, so, squinting against the sunlight, she tried to avoid contact with any of them as she made her way to the entrance.

The flurry of questions, far more personal and insensitive than any she had faced in the taxi, were hollered at her as she tried to maintain a straight line. Any hopes she'd had of the mourners already there not noticing her arrival were long gone, but Johnson was still shocked when a young woman emerged from the large oak doors and stared directly at her. The resemblance to McNeil was obvious and she was desperately thinking of what she was going to say to her by way of a greeting, when she suddenly looked over Johnson at her pursuers and called out: 'Have you no respect? Don't you think this woman has been through enough without you lot hounding her?'

Johnson smiled up at her weakly; this was certainly not the reaction she had expected. 'Thanks,' she muttered, as she made her way past and into the church.

'I'm Claire,' the woman said holding out her hand.

'Stella,' Johnson responded shaking it. 'You're…' she paused, suddenly aware this would be the first time she had ever uttered his forename. The closest she had got was those occasions when she prefixed McNeil with PC, as a way of teasing him with how junior he was. 'You're

Darren's sister.' The name felt alien on her lips, as though it belonged to someone else.

'Yes, come along, it's about to start. I've saved you a seat with us.'

Before she could begin to protest, Claire began leading her up the aisle of the packed church. Johnson regretted wearing heels; the loud clacking on the wooden floor doing more to announce her arrival than the reporters had. Faces turned towards her and she recognised a number from the station. They regarded her with a mixture of awkwardness and pity, all except for a blonde female constable whom Johnson only remembered was called Strachan because of the children's wildlife presenter she had watched growing up. The hatred in her eyes was clear and, in that moment, more than meeting his sister, Johnson realised she barely knew McNeil at all. She wondered what this woman was to him; it was evident she had some personal feelings for him but whether there had been anything between them she would never know.

Fortunately, sight of DSI Potter helped Johnson to regain her composure. Dressed in his full uniform, he offered her the slightest incline of the head, which might have appeared cold had it not been for the moment they'd shared in the family room at the hospital a week before. Much as she was frustrated with his inability to catch Brandt, and his insistence they follow procedure regarding her reintroduction to work, she would always be grateful for his kindness that day.

As they arrived at the front of the church, Johnson regarded the people sat on her pew. At the far end were two men of similar ages who she took to be McNeil's brothers, and next to Claire was an older woman. The guarded look she gave Johnson as she sat down was more than enough to confirm she was his mother. McNeil's coffin was mere feet from her, and she wondered who, with the absence of a father, had helped the brothers carry it into the chapel.

Johnson had no more time to settle because the minister approached the pulpit and began proceedings. It was the standard mix of hymns, readings and people sharing their personal experiences. McNeil's family were remarkably dignified throughout, which she was extremely grateful for. The more she heard about McNeil the more it was confirmed that she barely knew him, and it just added to the surreal feeling she had being there. As a consequence, the tears that she had believed would be expected of her didn't fall, but she did occasionally dab her eyes with a tissue to keep up the pretence.

Following the service, the congregation were led via a side door into the graveyard and to a plot that had been freshly dug. It was clear from the reaction of the mourners that this was the hardest part and, as McNeil's coffin was gently lowered into the ground, Johnson caught his mother glance sharply in her direction. She wondered how many unanswered questions they had about the reason for him being at her house that night. Of course, the tabloids had offered some speculation, whilst trying to maintain a false air of respectability. The fact was no one would ever know the truth, but Johnson hoped that McNeil had come around because he refused to accept her request to be patient.

She waited for the first people to start drifting away before making her move, planning to go to her flat and cancel her appointment with the police doctors. Perhaps even get away for a while; anything to escape all this. But Johnson had only taken a few steps when a firm but gentle hand on her arm caused her to stop.

'Let's find somewhere quiet to talk.' There was no element of request to what Claire said.

Johnson didn't reply but allowed herself to be led further into the church grounds. She wondered whether being berated by a member of his family might actually be a good thing. It wasn't as though it could make her guilt any worse, and she wished Claire would just come out with it.

'I know you were close,' she stated once they were sufficiently out of earshot. Johnson didn't know how to respond and so merely nodded. 'Darren told me about you...'

Oh, here goes, she thought.

'...he didn't want to, but I got it out of him. You see, he wanted to be a policeman since, well, since I can remember. He was so excited when he was accepted but then things started to change. He didn't want to admit it and tried to hide it from Mum who was super proud and couldn't stop herself telling everyone she met. But I saw it. He had so much good in him that he wanted to make a difference, a real difference.'

Johnson shuffled awkwardly on the spot, looking down at her heels which were beginning to sink in the soft soil. She didn't want to hear how she had not only cost him his life but, prior to that, his love for a job he had always wanted to do. She felt the urge to run and leave this all behind her.

'Late nights breaking up drunken fights and following up petty theft. It was draining him. But then you came along.' Johnson looked up suddenly, sure she must be misunderstanding Claire's words. 'Look, I'm not saying those murders were a good thing. Of course they weren't, they were awful. But you involving Darren changed him. I didn't know he was working on the case but when I challenged him on his apparent good mood, he couldn't help but spill the beans. Just the look in his eyes told me that he was finally doing something he considered important. He was scared he would get into trouble for telling me and made me promise I wouldn't tell Mum and our brothers but, having confided in me, he couldn't stop talking about it any time we met up or spoke on the phone.'

'What did he say?' Johnson couldn't help but be intrigued.

'Well, he refused to give any details. Even as kids, Darren would always insist on playing by the rules. But he just wanted to share how he was feeling about things. He was a bit up and down, you know, sometimes frustrated by the lack of progress that was being made, but he couldn't stop talking about you.'

'Me?'

'Yeah, the comments changed over the weeks. I could tell he was initially intimidated by you, perhaps even a little scared. Then he started talking about how knowledgeable you were. And then he stopped talking about you altogether. I knew then what had happened…'

'What?' Johnson wasn't sure she wanted to hear any of this, but the conversation was so different to what she had expected that she couldn't help but find herself interested.

'He was always like that,' Claire laughed, a little too falsely. 'We always knew when he fancied someone because he would suddenly stop talking about them. It was after that trip to Canterbury or wherever it was you both went. He came home and suddenly wanted to talk about anything but his work.'

'We weren't together,' Johnson said flatly.

'I know. Ever since we were small, I've been able to get the details out of him. He told me nothing happened in Kent and, as far as I know, nothing happened since. But then…'

'…but then he was at my house.' Johnson finished for her.

'Well, yes. Look, I genuinely don't want to pry…'

'…I didn't know he was coming around. He had never been there before, well except once when I was picking him up.'

Claire placed a hand on her shoulder. 'As I said, I don't want to pry. Like I said at the beginning, I know you two were close. I need your help.'

'Help?'

Claire grasped her other shoulder, her face now so close to Johnson that she could smell her perfume and stale cigarette smoke. But rather than remind her of her own nicotine craving, Johnson found herself transfixed by eyes that, on the one hand looked so familiar, but on the other, so different. There was a cold intensity there that was in stark contrast to the warmth McNeil's had, even when he was being serious. 'I need you to catch him,' she said, her voice almost a whisper.

Johnson tried to back away. 'You think I don't?! Do you know what that man did to me, do you know what he was going to do to me if…if…' She stopped ready for the stinging reminder of McNeil's sacrifice.

'Shh,' Claire soothed, in contrast to her tightening grip. 'You misunderstand me. Of course, I know you want to catch him.' She paused, taking in a deep breath. 'But understand this: you need to catch him, whatever it takes. Whatever it takes.' She waited until the implication of her words sank in before removing her hands and offering a false smile. 'We're all back to a pub near Mum's if you would like to join us.'

'I'm afraid I can't, I have an appointment.'

'Really?' Claire raised an eyebrow.

'Yes, as a matter of fact it's about me returning to work.'

'Good,' she nodded. 'Tell you what, let me text you the address in case you can make it later.'

Johnson moved to start walking away. 'Oh no, I don't think so. By the time I finish and then…'

Claire blocked her path. 'Let me text you the address,' she repeated coldly.

Johnson fumbled in her bag for her phone. 'It's a new number and I'm not sure I know it. If you just tell me the name of the pub, I'll remember it should I have time later.'

Claire grabbed the phone from her hands and turned her back to prevent it easily being retaken. 'I'll just text myself and then I can reply,' she said whilst punching her number into an empty message. 'Here,' she said a few moments later, handing back the phone before walking away.

Johnson remained there looking at the screen. There was no incoming message with the address for the reception. As she slipped her phone back in her bag, she suspected that it would never arrive, but that this wouldn't be the last time she heard from Claire McNeil.

Chapter Thirteen

Johnson was travelling to the police station in her Audi. She had picked it up after her appointment because she wanted her return to work to appear as normal as possible. The assessment of her physical and psychological capability had gone well, in so much as she had been passed as fit. However, as she sat in traffic, the red of the lights a blur in her tear-filled vision, she knew that lying her way through the latter examination had been a big risk. If she wasn't able to pull herself together by the time her colleagues saw her, she was likely to face a longer lay off than if she had been honest about the conflict of emotions she was still experiencing.

Having sat through McNeil's funeral, Johnson had been sure that she wouldn't attend the appointment, understanding that, much as she hated sitting around doing nothing, she wasn't able to be that cold, logical Detective Chief Inspector her team needed, especially at such a trying time for the force. But Claire's words had weighed heavily on her and she realised that she owed it not just to McNeil but to all those who loved him to find Brandt. Whilst things had not panned out anything like she had intended, the fact remained that it was Johnson who managed to break the cycle of apparently random killings with few clues to go on. She alone made the connection with the murder in St. Albans and continued to champion it in the face of scepticism. Had it not been for her, they would not have the image from the Abbey station that they were able to cross reference with the CCTV from the other locations. Therefore, Johnson had done whatever it took and hid from the psychologist the extent of her feelings whilst offering just enough of her pain to appear credible. For no matter how screwed up she really was, she believed they stood a better chance of catching Brandt with her on board.

The gate to the car park retracting again, signalling the arrival of a colleague, caused Johnson to stub her barely lit cigarette out and swipe her way into the station. She tried to walk with confidence as she headed down the corridor and into the duty area. Sergeant Andrews was in his usual position at the desk, filling out his log book, but glanced up to offer her a slight nod. She was about to return it when the cold edge to his eyes caused her to turn and head straight for the stairs up to CID. She stopped, wanting nothing more than to go back down and tell that jumped up prick that, rather than trying to add to her own sense of guilt, he should take a look at his own culpability. It had been him that she had sent DI Fisher to when they had been so short staffed following the first incident. With a whole train load of potential suspects for the stabbing of Sarah Donovan, Johnson had needed to spread out her resources and required someone in uniform to accompany her to Sarah's ex-boyfriend's house. If Andrews hadn't given her McNeil, just some useless plod instead, then perhaps things would have worked out differently.

But Johnson carried on her ascent, the more rational part of her reminding her that if she over-analysed every look given to her and then responded with an outburst, she would be back in her car before the engine had even a chance to cool. Fortunately, her welcome in CID was warmer. She was one of them and they looked after their own. Johnson had a reputation for being a bit of a hard-arse, but she knew her team respected her. She led from the front and wouldn't ask anyone to do something she wasn't prepared to do herself. The flurry of activity she witnessed before being spotted stopped and she was swamped with people enquiring how she was and offering their sympathies. There were no awkward questions similar to those the taxi driver and the journalists had posed her, just genuine warmth and concern. Johnson tried to sweep it away, partly through a desire to get down to work but mainly for fear that this outpouring of love for her may cause a bigger reaction than nasty shits like Andrews.

'Thank you, guys, honestly!' She called, pulling herself away after the final hug from the gathered group. 'Look, I don't want to sound ungrateful but let's get back to business, shall we? DC Hardy can brief me in my office as to where we've got up to.' She turned to go but something about the complete silence she was leaving behind caused her to pause. 'What is it?'

Nervous glances at each other greeted her question. 'The DSI said he wanted to see you as soon as you arrived.' Fisher's lanky frame emerged from the back of the group. It suddenly occurred to Johnson that this was the first time she had noticed him since her arrival.

'Don't worry, I'll go see him as soon as I'm up to speed.'

'Er, sorry, ma'am, he really was quite insistent.'

She knew from his defiant look that she would get nothing sensible from the others until she had been to see Potter. 'Fine,' she replied tersely and headed straight for his office.

She considered knocking but knew the commotion outside would have signalled her arrival so, instead, she burst in through the door.

'Good morning, Stella,' he said, shuffling some papers on his desk to imply he had been busy doing something.

'Guv, you wanted to see me?'

'Yes, please sit down.'

Johnson was irked by his apparent formality, as though their encounter last week had never happened, but did as requested.

'I understand you were passed fit for active duty yesterday.'

'Raring to go.' She tried on what she hoped would appear a warm smile.

'I've seen the report and it has noted some concerns.'

'Concerns, guv?'

'Yes, well physically you seem to be in surprisingly good shape, but the psychologist said that, although she could find no concrete reason not to pass fit, she was troubled by your keenness to get back to work, not helped by the fact you had scheduled it the same afternoon as McNeil's funeral.'

Johnson decided that the best response to this was to provide none at all.

'Perhaps I wouldn't have read too much into it had it not been for our… chat last week.'

'That's not fair, guv!' Johnson could feel her cheeks flush with a mixture of embarrassment and anger. 'It was the morning after, and I was… I was…'

'No, Stella, what I am saying is that it was understandable given the circumstances. Perfectly understandable. What I am finding hard to believe is that in a matter of a week you have got over the terrible trauma you suffered.'

'Who said I have got over it?' Johnson sat bolt upright in her chair. Much as she wanted to show herself ready to work, she didn't want this. Irrespective of her personal feelings for McNeil, she had been attacked in her own home, stripped and tied to the bed and had to watch a colleague of hers die in front of her. She doubted anyone could get over that, especially not in the space of a week.

'You did,' Potter replied flatly, sifting through the papers on his desk to find a copy of the report. Then he read out, 'I now just want to move on and put all this behind me.'

Whatever it takes, Claire's words rang in her head once more. 'I didn't mean it like that,' she said quietly.

'Look, I don't doubt your sincerity but, regardless of the report's overall judgement, I need to know that returning to work is the best thing for you, Stella.'

Tears started welling in her eyes again. But she would not allow herself to be shamed by them; Potter's concern, however misguided she found it, was something that needed to be addressed. She could tell him what it had been like to be sat alone in her hotel room, waiting for news of Brandt's capture that never came. She could tell him how awful it had been to return home yesterday, to find what had happened there had been scrubbed away as though it had never occurred. More than this, she wanted to ask him how it was fucking possible in 2018 for a wanted serial killer to simply disappear without a trace. She wanted to know what the hell he and the others had been doing over the last week whilst she had been lying awake at night unable to stop the sobs that wracked her body.

'I need to be here,' she said finally.

Potter nodded slowly. 'Okay then. Look, something's come through that I want you to look into.'

Johnson's eyes lit up. This could be the breakthrough they required. She snatched the piece of paper he held in her direction, skimming over it in an effort to absorb the main points as quickly as possible. Confused, she started again and read it more carefully. 'Guv, there's a mistake here.' Potter's face remained expressionless. 'This can't have anything to do with him, just look where it is…'

'This is a different case, Stella, but one I need you to look into.'

'What the fuck?'

'DCI Johnson, whilst I am... sensitive to how things are at the moment, that outburst was way out of line.'

She would be damned if she was going to apologise. How could he do this to her? Of all people, he must understand her need to catch Brandt. He had even spoken about his guilt about not stopping her putting herself in danger. 'You can't do this, guv!'

'I'm afraid I can, and I have to do what I think is right. The report clears you for duty, but it is my decision what duty that is. I need not tell you how important it is we catch Jeffrey Brandt and I won't do anything I think may jeopardise the investigation.' He crossed his arms. 'What's more I don't think it would be healthy for you to be involved now.'

'This is bullshit though,' she cried, waving the piece of paper. 'This is some micky mouse drug related thing that should be given to one of the DCs.'

'We're a bit stretched at the moment.'

The reasonableness of Potter's tone made Johnson want to lean over the desk and smash his face in.

'Take it or leave it. No one would blame you if you realised... erm, decided that this was all too soon. It's not as though you haven't accrued enough holiday that you still need to take.'

She couldn't resist the urge to slam the door on her way out, despite knowing that Potter would somehow use it as justification that he had made the right decision. The way the detectives, so welcoming when she had arrived, busied themselves as she stalked across the room, was all the confirmation she needed that they had known she wouldn't be returning to work on the Brandt case.

Having unsuccessfully tried to calm herself on the way back down the stairs, she headed straight for the car park. She needed a cigarette and a chance to think this through. To suggest she was livid with Potter would be an understatement, but she wouldn't give him the satisfaction of just driving out of there. That way, even if she did subsequently return to work, she would never be allowed on the case. Her only option was to prove him wrong; follow his orders and demonstrate that his reservations were unwarranted. Although Potter was discreet, she remembered the odd indication he had given her of the intense pressure he was under by the top brass. She didn't need the furore the attack on her had created in the press for her to imagine how much greater that must be now. If there were no further developments, it wouldn't be long before he was begging her to be back on the case.

Johnson re-entered the station, burying her anger and frustration under the knowledge that she was doing the right thing in the circumstances. 'Andrews,' she called loudly across the duty area. She had to bite her tongue when he continued writing his sentence before looking up.

'Get me one of your boys, I need to take him on a little errand.' She was sure he couldn't fail to see the parallels with when he had provided McNeil. He was opening his mouth to respond to her but something about her expression caused him to turn away instead.

'Fiona, go and see if PC Barnes has finished his break.'

Johnson had continued to glare at Andrews but stopped when the person she saw out of the corner of her eye failed to move. It was the woman who had been eyeballing her at the funeral.

'Problem?' Andrews asked.

'No, Sarge,' she replied coldly. Without further response she walked slowly towards the staff canteen area.

Moments later, with Andrews seemingly busy filling out his log book once more, and Johnson wondering whether she should find Fiona Strachan and ask what the fuck her problem was, a tall black male emerged holding a Styrofoam cup of coffee. 'You wanted me, Sarge?'

'DCI Johnson needs someone to accompany her on a case.' Much as she still regarded Andrews as a pencil-pushing little twat, she couldn't help but admire his professionalism.

Barnes' face lit up. 'Certainly, sir,' he replied with such enthusiasm that if he had then snapped to attention and saluted, it wouldn't have come as a great surprise. 'Hello, ma'am,' he said approaching her. 'I'm Simon, but everyone calls me John.' He seemed uncomfortable with Johnson's blank look. 'You know John Barnes the footballer? World Cup 1990 and that rap?'

'Let's go,' she said simply, turning on her heels and heading for the police cars. She couldn't help but smile when he headed straight for one of the marked Ford Focus panda cars. 'No, PC Barnes, we're undercover,' she teased.

'Really?' he responded, again taking on that look of an excited child. His face dropped. 'But I'm in uniform. Have I got time to go and get changed?'

Johnson shrugged. 'If you like.' She was in no hurry and would use the time to spark up another cigarette. Much as she still was angry about what Potter had done, at least this was better than hanging around at the rented flat that she had already taken such a dislike to. She was also grateful for the fact Barnes appeared nothing like McNeil. It wasn't so much the fact that they looked entirely different; even on their first encounter McNeil had displayed a maturity that belied his relative inexperience. Normally someone like Barnes would drive Johnson mad, but his persona was a welcome contrast and she promised herself that she would try and be patient with him.

'Wow,' he said, returning a few minutes later in jeans and black hoody, regarding the BMW M4 Johnson was stood next to. 'My uncle had one of those, although it was an older generation than this. I think it was an M3. Went like shit off a…' He paused suddenly. 'Sorry, ma'am.'

'Shit off a shovel?'

'Yeah, yeah, that's it!' His look of guilt instantly fell from his face.

* * *

Moments later they pulled out of the car park; Johnson unable to resist applying just enough throttle to provoke a squeal of wheel spin. 'Where are we going?'

'St. Ann's.'

'Okay,' he replied nervously. Nottingham was famous for its gun crime, but the reality was it tended to be localised. For most people the city was a nice place in which to live but, similar to London, there were certain pockets where things were unpleasant. St. Ann's, to the east, was notorious for this and Johnson had spent quite a bit of time there in her early years in CID. This was one of the reasons why she had been so affronted when Potter had given her the case. Crimes that warranted their attention in St. Ann's were usually gun or drug related and, aside from muggings and burglary, they were often restricted to the people involved in illegal activities. Naturally, Johnson had applied herself diligently to these cases, but they weren't the ones she looked forward to investigating when she got promoted. She had joined the force, in much the way Claire had described McNeil's motives, to protect those people who led ordinary, decent lives. Of course, there were plenty of such people who happened to live in St. Ann's, but experience had taught Johnson that, more often than not, the victims of crime in this area, even if they happened to have a clean record themselves, were unwilling to cooperate with the police. She had initially put it down to fear of reprisal but had come to see it more as some kind of fucked up code that many of them followed, as though the authorities were worse than the criminals. Whilst Johnson accepted that the police had to take some responsibility in the creation of this situation, she would leave it to the community liaison officers and other do-gooders in the force to try and address that.

The crime scene was as Johnson expected. A rental house that had been used as a drug den; its unkempt garden and peeling front door barely any worse than the properties surrounding it, but squalid and bare inside. Each room was given over to mattresses and tatty armchairs which, by the looks of the debris scattered, had largely been in use when the shooting had taken place. It had only been the noisy fleeing of its occupants that had caused a local resident to anonymously alert the emergency services. The ambulance arrived to find a young white male lying unconscious following a shot to his abdomen. Even Barnes' enthusiasm waned as they made their way door to door, unsuccessful in their attempts to gain any further information as to what had happened or who else they might speak to.

The house itself was registered to a woman who had yet to be tracked down, so, with little more that could be done there, they headed for the hospital to check on the condition of the victim. Johnson couldn't help but wonder whether Potter's insensitivity at providing her with a case that, not only had required her to take a new recruit like she had with McNeil, but also would see her back at the Queen's Medical Centre, was deliberate. Perhaps she was right; this was all part of a test to see whether she was genuinely ready to return to work. Nevertheless, it did not stop the apprehension she felt arriving there. Fortunately, they would be visiting a different ward, but she was sure she would be recognised by some of the staff. As long as it wasn't either of the nurses she'd had run-ins with, it wouldn't be so bad, but it did make her wonder why Barnes had not mentioned what had happened to her.

'Are you aware of who I am?' She asked as she pulled into a parking space.

'Ma'am?'

'I mean, do you know what happened?'

'Of course, ma'am, and I'm really sorry. I didn't like to mention it before and seem like I was prying. You seemed all ready for business, so I thought it best to just focus on what we were doing.' The concern was evident in his voice.

'It's fine and, to be honest, I'm grateful for that. Er,' she paused, wondering whether she really wanted to ask the next question. 'Did you know PC McNeil?'

'Darren? Yes, I knew him. It's not as though we trained together; he started a good while before me, but we went on some of the same jobs.'

'Were you friends?'

'Er, yeah sort of. We didn't really socialise or anything but we both went out for the usual Friday or Saturday night drinks if we weren't on shift. He stopped coming to those though…'

'Why was that?'

'I dunno, it was after he started working with your lot. I reckoned he had started going out with them instead.' Johnson wasn't surprised by the old notion of the plain clothes/uniform divide but, as far as she was aware, CID didn't specifically socialise unless celebrating a particular occasion. She always assumed that it was because they tended to be older and were therefore more likely to have families.

'How do you feel about what happened?'

'Well, I guess it seemed normal.' Barnes must have noticed the shock on Johnson's face and gave an embarrassed laugh. 'Oh shit, sorry, I thought you meant him not going out with us anymore. You mean what happened to him? Well, it's dreadful really. I guess we know it's a risk of the job, but you never really expect it to happen to one of you, do you?'

'And what do people think of me?' Johnson was surprised she cared, let alone had enough courage to ask the question.

'Well, of course it's terrible what happened to you too…'

'No, I mean, do they blame me?'

'Jesus, no, why would they?'

'What about PC Strachan?'

101

Barnes shifted uncomfortably in his seat. 'That's a bit different though, ma'am.' Johnson waited, using silence to encourage him to qualify his statement. 'She had a bit of a thing for Darren.'

'Were they an item?' She instantly regretted using a term that made her sound so old.

'I don't think so but…'

'But what?' Johnson failed to hide the urgency in her voice.

'Well, things could get a little messy late on when we were out.' He paused, thinking. 'Look, I don't know whether anything happened between them, it's just that Fiona kept talking about him no longer coming and even texted him a few times when we were out to try and get him to join us.'

Johnson didn't know why she cared so much. As Barnes had said, McNeil had stopped socialising with uniform once he had started working with her, so it's not as though anything that happened between the two of them wasn't before she had started developing feelings for him. It didn't stop the faint pang of jealousy she was experiencing. They both clearly had a past but the thought of him with someone else only served to highlight the fact they had done nothing more than kiss.

With regrets of their night in Canterbury entering her mind once more, she opened the car door and started marching towards the hospital entrance, making Barnes run in order to catch up. She regretted broaching the subject and was determined that any remaining conversation between the two of them would be limited to the details of the case they were investigating.

Having been directed to the right area they were stopped just as they were about to enter the victim's room. 'You can't go in there!' An officious voice caused them to turn around. Fortunately, it wasn't a nurse Johnson recognised, and by her expression it appeared she didn't know who she was either.

'DCI Johnson, and this is PC Barnes,' she said, trying to hide her irritation. 'We're here to see Craig King regarding the incident last night.'

'You can't go in,' the nurse repeated, albeit a little more calmly. 'He's only just waking up following surgery.'

'Please, madam, we just need to ask him a couple of quick questions,' Barnes said, flashing her with a dazzlingly smile. 'It really was a nasty incident…'

'Well okay then,' she said with a good-natured huff. 'But just two minutes mind, and I'll be in there to remove you.'

'Two minutes,' he said.

* * *

Despite his apparent grogginess, Craig King instantly recognised Johnson and Barnes for what they were. 'It was nothing,' he mumbled. 'Just a misunderstanding.'

'What was nothing?' Johnson asked, stepping forward to indicate to Barnes that, despite his success in gaining them entry, she was going to take it from here.

'What happened to me.' The fear was evident in his tone.

'Look, Craig, we're here to help. Just tell us who did this to you.'

'I er… I don't know. I didn't see who it was.'

'And yet you said it was a misunderstanding.'

'A misunderstanding. Yeah, that was it, just a misunderstanding.'

'How do you know it was a misunderstanding?'

'What?'

'You just said that you didn't see who shot you, so how do you know that they didn't mean to?'

'What? Did I just say that?' Panic was rising in his voice. 'It's the drugs you see… No, no I don't mean drugs like that. No, I don't do anything like that.' Johnson took a deliberate look up and down at his bare arms, taking in their tell-tale puncture wounds from frequent needle use. 'I meant the drugs, the hospital drugs they've given me here,' he continued weakly. 'The codeine or morphine or whatever the fuck they've given me has scrambled my memory. To tell the truth, I can't remember what happened. I don't even remember what I was doing there.'

'Really?' Barnes said, stepping forward. Johnson grabbed his arm and shot him a look that told him not to bother.

'Get some rest, Mr King, we'll be returning tomorrow morning.'

* * *

Johnson was soon back in her office with the blinds drawn, filling out her report from the morning. She had no appetite for it but knew she could string it out for the rest of the day undisturbed. The awkwardness that had followed her meeting with Potter had remained as she re-entered CID, and her decision to maintain a low profile was as much for their benefit as it was for hers.

PC Barnes had seemed genuinely disappointed on their return journey to the station and Johnson wondered how many similar experiences he would have to go through before he had the enthusiasm knocked out of him. She tried to cheer him up with reassurances that it was impossible to help those who refused it, but she understood his frustration, having gone through the same thing many times in her career. That's why the stabbings had captured her imagination so much, and not just through her desire to protect the people she had taken an oath to serve. It had been a game of wits, pitting her skills against those she was chasing. She hadn't known it at the time, but it somehow now made sense that it had been done by an ex-copper. The arrogance he had displayed by taunting them with the links to his previous crimes could only come from someone who was either deranged and destined to slip up, or someone who knew their investigative methods inside out. And yet Johnson had found the chink in his armour. She didn't fully understand why things had gone so wrong in St. Albans that he had sought to distance himself from what he had done there, but she had managed to exploit it all the same.

Johnson needed to be there when the next slip up came, because someone couldn't disappear completely. No matter how well planned and how carefully executed, there was always a trace; however feint. She continued to fill out the pointless report about a pointless case in the hope that, in doing so, it might take her one step closer to the action.

Chapter Fourteen

Within hours of arriving in Benidorm, Brandt already hated the place. It hadn't taken him long upon realising Franklin could literally be his passport to the continent, that it would be his destination. For someone who didn't speak a word of any foreign language, Benidorm, with its tens of thousands of British holiday makers and ex-pats, seemed perfect. Yet he hadn't expected them to be quite so fucking British down there. The place, which had seemed picturesque in the few images he had seen of it in the past, was actually more like Blackpool, just with decent sunshine. Everywhere he turned there was a bar with some tacky English name advertising pints for €2 and cafés with fried breakfasts for €3. He tried to reassure himself that hiding in plain sight was better than sticking out like a sore thumb as a foreigner in a place full of locals, but it was the Brits' other obsession, besides cheap booze and increasing their cholesterol, that troubled him. Despite them costing many times the price back home, everyone seemed to be walking round with a British newspaper under their arm.

Under other circumstances, his exploits being front page news would have pleased him, but here it was as though every person he saw was carrying his wanted poster around. Not satisfied with speculation that he was at large back in England, he took immediate steps to alter his appearance. Shunning the main hotels because of their likely insistence on wanting to see a passport on check-in, he found himself a villa in a small complex on the edge of town run by a Spanish family. Satisfied that he would be relatively safe there, his next stop had been at an electrical store to purchase a set of hair clippers. Alarmed by his pale scalp he had worn a hat for the first few days when in public, spending time on his balcony back at the villa to gradually tan it, along with the rest of his features. It had taken him a couple of days to hitchhike his way down to the Spanish coast, so he already had a head start with the beard he had intended growing.

The problem for Brandt had been that as soon as he felt less conspicuous about his appearance, he started reflecting more and more on what had happened. That he had managed to make his escape wasn't just a relief to him; it was also a boost to his fragile ego. He had underestimated how close the police had come to identifying him but remaining at least one step ahead of them confirmed to Brandt that he hadn't overestimated his own skills. Although his intention had been to kill Johnson, the news that she had survived didn't concern Brandt. Given that he had been denied the opportunity to fully demonstrate how wrong that vicious newspaper article had been, he reasoned that her being forced to live with the consequences of his visit was perhaps a more fitting punishment.

But with that came the realisation that he too had lost his purpose in life. The suicidal thoughts Brandt had held for many years hadn't returned, but one day had started to drift into the next without any real meaning. It wasn't as though he felt he could move on because Franklin's car had yet to be discovered. He had read snippets in the press about other lines of enquiry that he assumed were an oblique reference to Franklin, but Brandt was still the focus of all their attention.

He slowly became obsessed with how he was being portrayed. The downside of selecting a villa designed to cater for the few Spanish tourists who braved the British dominated Benidorm, was that the television didn't show any of the English channels. After a couple of days of going from shop to shop to collect the various newspapers that were available over there, he purchased himself a second-hand laptop and took advantage of the complex's Wi-Fi connection. Brandt didn't consider himself an IT specialist, but he had embraced the computer revolution in his early career for the advantages it gave his investigations. Whilst limited to programmes that aided his work, in the years after his wife left, he became more adept at the wider applications. His use of the internet had mainly centred around accessing pornography, but as his tastes had become darker and more extreme, he had learned a lot about how to disguise the trail one left online. The last thing he would have wanted whilst still in the force would be for his colleagues to find out about his proclivities.

Yet he didn't once access explicit material on his new laptop. He didn't consider that it may have something to do with watching sexual acts no longer being sufficient for his evolving desires, instead convincing himself that he was putting pleasure aside until his work was done. The benefit of having the internet was that it allowed him to see the stories he had missed in the time he had spent getting to Benidorm. Although it had taken a day for the print editions to catch up, news of what he had done had broken whilst he had still been in Belgium. The police had been quick to exploit the publicity in the hope it would aid them in finding him.

Brandt had never expected people to understand his actions, so his portrayal as an abomination had been expected. In the days that followed, questions had been raised about his motives and, although none of them were correct, Brandt was happy that there were no longer suggestions as to his sexuality. He guessed they would get to his wife eventually but if there was one thing he knew about Susan, it was that she would be hating the negative attention and would be doing her best to avoid it, even in the face of vast sums of money being offered for her to sell her story.

But as the week wore on Brandt became frustrated by how quickly things changed to other news. He knew that there was only a limited amount that could be said about what had happened, but he also took it as symptomatic of the problems in society that his actions had been trying to address. That the country appeared to be able to move on so fast only reaffirmed his belief that it had become too desensitised; too complacent. It upset Brandt that there was little he could do about it stuck in his Spanish villa, but he knew that there was one card left to play. His abduction of Franklin had initially been to aid his own getaway and then about trying to deflect some of the attention away from him. He had wanted to conceal his death to allow him sufficient time to get to Spain, but now he yearned for Franklin to be found. Not only would it serve to bring his actions to the forefront of the news once more but the revelations in the suicide note would help to keep them there.

Brandt barely paid any attention to the photographs taken of Johnson at the copper's funeral. He had seen beyond that cold, focused exterior and knew the real person underneath. Instead, he was busy looking into things like the dark web and how to, not only conceal IP addresses, but make them appear like they had come from somewhere else. It would have been easier for him to telephone but aside from the fact he didn't speak a word of French, there was no such thing as a truly anonymous call. People bought cheap pay as you go phones over the counter for use as burners; discarded as soon as they had served their purpose. What many of them failed to realise is that the number may not be directly associated with them but the signal could be traced like any other. It did not matter that it had been subsequently switched off, the police would be able to track the call to the specific phone mast that it had used. Having gone to all the effort of making it appear like he had remained in the British Isles or, at the very least, heading towards central Europe, the last thing he wanted was to potentially give away his current location.

It took many hours of research for him to feel confident enough to risk sending an email from the new account he had created, but still he decided it would be safer to send it from one of Benidorm's internet cafés.

Walking into the shop, Brandt portrayed himself as the typically incompetent computer user that characterised much of his generation, he had once heard them referred to as silver surfers. He even asked for the person in charge to help him open up the web browser, despite the clear instructions typed on a laminated sheet in both English and Spanish. Not only would this cover his tracks if, somehow, someone was able to trace it back to here but the manager, anxious that he might be called on to perform every basic function Brandt needed, then found something at the opposite end of the café that required his immediate attention.

He didn't know why Franklin's car had remained undiscovered for so long. Perhaps the silt on the lake bed had given way and it had slipped further in, meaning that the roof was no longer visible. Regardless, that it seemingly now fell on him to reveal it allowed Brandt to feel a sense of control again. Once he had performed the various actions he had learned to alter the IP address to one in Belgium, he jumped onto his trusted Google maps and worked out roughly where he had driven the X5 off the small road that went around the lake. Remembering to keep his description of the distance in metric units, he began composing his email.

Chapter Fifteen

Johnson felt like shit the next morning. She had barely slept, not helped by a text she had received from Claire shortly after she had got back to the flat. Presented as innocently as possible, it apologised for forgetting to send the whereabouts of the reception following the funeral and enquired how she was doing. However, Johnson knew the real meaning behind it and, deciding not to play games, she responded that she was back at work. 'Good' was the simple reply that followed. That one single word spoke volumes. Johnson was under no illusion that it meant Claire was pleased that she was starting the process of rebuilding her life. It was a prompt that they were relying on her to catch McNeil's killer, perhaps even a reminder that Johnson was responsible for what happened.

Driving into the station, the belief that she had held yesterday that the case she had been given about the shooting in St. Ann's would somehow see her return to the fold, had eroded away. She would keep to her promise of revisiting the victim but knew they would continue to gain nothing of use from him. She knew that rather than reconsider his decision to hide the identity of his attacker, the likelihood was that he would have used the intervening hours to come up with a better story for what had happened and why he had been in a drug den in the first place. The best she could do was to tie this one up as quickly as possible, present her findings to DSI Potter and wait for the next pointless case to be sent her way.

Entering the duty area, she approached Sergeant Andrews. 'Is PC Barnes available again today?' She hoped that her phrasing it as a request rather than a demand, along with her more pleasant tone, wouldn't go unnoticed.

What she hadn't expected was his uneasy expression. 'Are you going up first?'

'No, we're just going to crack on with it,' she replied breezily before hesitating. 'Why?'

'I just think you might like to go on up to CID before you do.'

Johnson was about to ask what the hell had got into him but there was something about the intensity of Andrews' stare that made her feel uncomfortable. Without responding, she turned and headed for the stairs.

Punching in the number, she could see most of the team were huddled round a computer. Nothing terribly out of the ordinary except for the way they all looked up guiltily as she marched through the door.

'What?' She barked.

'DCI Johnson, you'd better come in here,' Potter called from the entrance to his office. She shot the others a look of irritation as she followed his instruction.

'Look, I'm about to go and see him now but, I tell you, it's a complete waste of time. He's just going to…'

'Sit down, Stella,' he interrupted.

She plonked herself in the chair with a huff. 'What is it with all the weirdness today? I kind of expected it yesterday, what with it being my first day but first Andrews and now…'

'Franklin's body's been found.'

'His body? Where?'

'Belgium, near a place called Ghent. Not too far from Brussels.'

'Shit, I bloody knew it!' She stood up and started pacing back and forth in the room. 'I knew he couldn't still be in Britain. He's a loner, he would have been spotted by now…'

'Hold on Stella. There's more.'

She stopped and glared at Potter. She hated the way he always seemed so calm, especially the way he always took so long to explain anything.

'It looks like suicide. Shot himself in the head as he rolled the car into a lake.'

'What? But that doesn't make sense. Why would you kill yourself and hide the body?'

'He left a note. In it he talks about his shame at what he's done and how he is responsible for what happened.'

'Let me see it!'

'No, Stella!' Potter said firmly. 'I'm only telling you this because I didn't want you harassing the others until they told you. We're on it, okay?'

'Harassing them? Fuck's sake, guv, they're my team! Let me run with this, I'm sure I'll find something that will lead me to Brandt. He's behind all this, I know he is.'

Potter put his heads in his hands and sighed. 'This is the problem, Stella. You're personally involved now. Of course you are; it's not your fault. If I show you the note, you're going to fit it into your pre-conceived notion that he's the ringleader in all this. What's more dangerous is that you'll get the others thinking the same as you.'

'Pre-conceived notion? He was fucking there! Brandt was the one who knocked me out. Brandt was the one who stripped me and tied me up. It was Brandt who climbed on top of me and started… started to…' Even in her rage, Johnson couldn't bring herself to say how he had molested her. 'He killed McNeil,' she added quietly.

Moments of silence followed with Johnson staring at Potter imploringly and him unsure how to continue without completely destroying what was left of their relationship.

He doubted Johnson would forgive him for what he was about to say but he knew it was the right thing to do. He would not allow her to be put in harm's way again and risk another officer dying. 'This case is about more than just you and PC McNeil.'

Johnson slumped back into the chair, wounded. She thought the pain she had experienced was as bad as it could get but this was somehow worse. It was one thing to believe she was too emotionally involved to lead on this, but to have the one man she looked up to be so dismissive about what had happened, hurt more than anything she could imagine. She didn't want to talk to him anymore; she couldn't even bring herself to look at him. But to leave now would mean going back to her pointless case and allowing this huge injustice to go unanswered. She would go above his head, say whatever it took to get rid of him and then she could focus on what needed to be done; catching that bastard. She could say he made an inappropriate advance towards her. That was it, she could say he took advantage of her when she came out of hospital. She could say he touched her in the car whilst she was still only wearing the hospital gown, and that he had booked the hotel, so he could come around and have sex with her whilst she was in a vulnerable state.

But she knew she couldn't say any of it. Much as she hated Potter at that very moment, she wouldn't destroy him like this. She didn't know why he was being so cruel to her, but she wouldn't allow her actions to undermine all those women who were battling against genuine sexual harassment. Much as she knew she could be as convincing as necessary, especially in the current climate of Time's Up and the scandals that had rocked the media industry, she couldn't live with herself if she became just as bad as those scumbags who used their position of power to prey on women.

Whatever it takes. Those haunting words causing her to question whether she was allowing her sense of right and wrong to deflect her from her true moral responsibility. But there was another way.

'I can't do this anymore,' she said quietly, tears streaming down her face. Potter got up and walked round the desk. His arms opened as though he was going to try and comfort her, but he hesitated. Johnson wondered for a moment whether he suspected what she had been contemplating doing.

'I understand,' he said, awkwardly folding them. 'More than you can appreciate.'

'I need to get out of here.' She still couldn't bring herself to look at Potter directly.

'Of course, of course,' the relief in his voice was sickening. 'Take as long as you need.'

'You mentioned holidays I've accrued.'

'Yes, absolutely. I'll sign them off. No one need know you're not fit for duty. Don't worry about that other case, I'll put someone else on it.' He lowered his voice. 'By the time you're ready to come back we'll have Brandt and we can all try and put this behind us.'

She shook her head but managed to stop herself challenging the hope with which he had delivered those last few words. It wasn't so much the, almost flippant, suggestion that she might excuse the things he had said to her today, but the belief that they would just simply move on from McNeil's death.

Twice in two days she had to march across the CID area in a vain attempt to hide her bitter emotions. How could she be expected to lead the team again in the future when they had seen her like this? As she reached the duty area, she wanted to thank Andrews for showing her the kind of compassion that had escaped her colleagues upstairs, but his sympathetic nod in her direction told her nothing needed to be said. Relieved that it helped speed her departure, she didn't then stop to light a cigarette as she entered the car park, choosing instead to break her rule about smoking in the Audi.

As she waited for the security gate's slow progress in opening, she couldn't help but wonder when she would next see the inside of Nottingham Central Police Station. But that didn't matter; nothing did, except for the one thing she must do. *Whatever it takes.*

Chapter Sixteen

Brandt felt better than he had at any moment since leaving England. Actually, that wasn't true, sat in the back of the car whilst Franklin blew his head off had been pretty special, but this was a longer lasting thrill. Sitting on his balcony allowing the early morning rays of sunshine to warm his face, he tried to imagine the flurry of activity that would have greeted his email. He wondered whether the Belgian authorities had informed their contacts in the UK police before following up the message's claim of knowing the whereabouts of Franklin's car. Brandt had been careful not to display too much knowledge of what had been seen by the phantom emailer, but just enough that they would realise which vehicle was being referred to. He had needed to keep it simple anyway because he was relying on an online translator to convert it into convincing French.

Buoyed by this, and in the knowledge that it would be a few hours yet until anything made it onto the news sites, he headed into town. Brandt made an instant judgement on his arrival in Benidorm, no doubt not helped by tiredness, that he didn't like it very much and had limited his time in public to running necessary errands; convincing himself that he needed to lay low. Now that his appearance was as altered as he was likely to manage without cosmetic surgery, it seemed time to establish whether he could find something of a life for himself there.

That it was fairly quiet in the Old Town, the more cosmopolitan area that was less attractive to the beer-swilling holiday makers, reminded him of Rudyard Kipling's phrase about it only being mad dogs and Englishmen who went out in the midday sun. Kipling may have been referring to India but with the early summer temperatures well into the 30s, Brandt could see the parallels. Not that he didn't like the heat; he and his wife had gone to a number of tropical destinations in the early part of their marriage. She used to like lying on a sun lounger reading a trashy romance novel whereas Brandt, who found it hard to relax, would go off exploring.

With memories of the good times prominent in Brandt's mind, he made his way through the tight streets and down to the Mal Pas Beach. Without the shade provided by the various buildings, the sweat was beginning to pour off him and the lure of the blue Mediterranean Sea was too strong. He hadn't brought any swimming trunks but figured that his underpants were respectable enough and, leaving the rest of his clothes in a heap just out of the water's reach, he waded in. The coolness of it was a pleasant shock to his system, especially once it reached his midriff, but nothing like the chill he had experienced venturing into British waters when on holiday as a child.

Happy memories once again and, after a while splashing around, Brandt started to feel hungry. It had been an expensive first few days in Benidorm, having bought himself the essentials for the villa, along with his laptop. However, he had calculated that his money should now last him a good number of months before he needed to find some form of employment. He guessed he would end up with bar work but the idea of having to remain sober whilst surrounded by all that alcohol didn't really appeal. He figured that if he learnt the basics of Spanish, he could maybe even do some mini-cabbing. Much as he didn't like the working-class Brits, ferrying them to and from the characterless bars would be better than having to serve them their €2 pints and shots of sambuca all evening.

Despite his growing appetite, Brandt waited on the beach for his pants to dry sufficiently for him to put on his clothes. He was going to sit on one of the sun loungers when he noticed the sign advertising the cost. Another day, when he was better kitted out, he may spend some time down here, but the lure of a late lunch was proving too strong. He did stay a little longer though, and could overhear snippets of conversations confirming the Spanish tended to favour this over the Levante Beach preferred by the Brits, attached to the New Town. Looking around, he found that many of the women were sunbathing topless. Moving to the back of the beach so he could observe them from behind the relative safety offered by his dark glasses, whilst appearing to just be looking out to sea, he could feel himself beginning to become aroused. It did not matter to him that many of the pairs of breasts on show belonged to older women and, subjectively, were not that attractive; it was the voyeuristic act itself that was giving him a thrill.

He found himself thinking back to DCI Johnson's house. Until now his recollections of that evening had surrounded all the things that had gone wrong, but there had been a few minutes of genuine pleasure. He remembered quickly dragging her inside and shutting the front door. With her lying unconscious in the hallway, and without that icy intense stare that had so disturbed him whenever he had seen her on television, he was fully able to appreciate her beauty. She was older than his other female victims but could see that maturity suited her and guessed she had grown more attractive during her adult life.

He had known that he should tie her up as quickly as possible before she woke but, having removed her bra, he sat her up, so he could observe her breasts in their most natural state. They had been perfect; sizeable enough but pert and with inviting round, pink nipples. At that moment he had wanted nothing more than to pull down her knickers and be inside her, but he knew she needed to be conscious for that act. It wasn't so much that he had wanted to feel the movement of her body, as he had done with the girl in St. Albans, he needed her to know that her malicious claims of homosexuality were false. Whilst tying her up he had realised that all the anger and hatred had melted away and it was with regret that he knew he had to kill her. He couldn't allow compassion to get in the way of business, but he had planned to make her death as quick and relatively painless as possible.

And yet things had changed when she opened her eyes. The initial look of horror had been as welcomed as it was expected, but then came the defiance. He could feel his power slipping away with every passing moment and every word she spoke about knowing who he was and what he had done in St. Albans. He had managed to ride it out and focus on the physicality of their situation. He had planned on speaking to her longer; having her accept the necessity of what was going to happen. Instead he climbed on top of her knowing at that point that killing her would be easy, but he would only do that once he had fully satisfied himself.

But he hadn't.

That nosey little cunt had disturbed them, no doubt hoping for his own little fumble that evening. He was pleased he was dead and only wished he had been in the same room to witness him bleed out like a stuck pig.

As Brandt continued to regard those Spanish breasts on a beach far from Nottingham, he no longer felt aroused. None of them were as good as Johnson's and, even if they were, just sitting there looking at them was nothing compared to what he would have, should have, done to her. As he got up and trudged off towards the new town in search of his cheap all-day breakfast, he knew at that point that he would not be able to settle in his new home until he was compensated for his loss.

Chapter Seventeen

Johnson could feel a calmness descend as she drove to the Channel Tunnel. It wasn't just that she had put Potter and all his bullshit behind her, she felt she was on the right trail. Although determined to see Franklin's note in order to evaluate its full contents, she had gained enough of an understanding to know that the police believed it to confirm that Brandt was still in England. Yet she knew differently. Every ounce of the intuition she had honed over her career was telling her she was following his tracks. For the first time since that awful night she had a singularity of purpose. For now, she could lock away the pain that was inside her and focus on the thing she could change. Potter and his lap-dog DI Fisher were conspiring to fuck up their chances of catching the real criminal and she was the only one who could stop that from happening. She would find Brandt and bring him to justice. *Whatever it takes.*

The serenity that had escaped her when believing she was doing the right thing by following Potter's menial detective work in St Ann's, allowed her to sleep during the short train ride to Calais. Little did she know that her quarry had done the same but, as she was awoken by the swinging back of the huge internal doors, she felt refreshed and ready for the remainder of her journey. She hadn't been told the exact location of where Franklin's car had been discovered but there was only one major lake near Ghent and, besides, it was no doubt now in whatever compound the police there used.

Johnson had been academically able at school and her mother had been desperate for her to be the first in their family to go to university. When she learned of her desire to enter the police force she had begged her to wait until she could join as a graduate. But much as Johnson enjoyed the success that exams had brought her, she equally knew she possessed the talent to rise through the ranks just as fast if she had a three-year head start. With her 18th birthday falling early in the academic year she was still studying for her A Levels, she made her application and began her training as soon as she could after sitting her final paper. So focused was she on her new job that she didn't even go back into school to collect her results, which were two As and a B in Biology, Psychology and French respectively. And it was her knowledge in that latter subject that she would draw on, all these years later, to ensure she would get the information she required. She doubted that the Belgian authorities, upon seeing her warrant card, would seek to check that she had been sent over from Britain, but her experiences abroad had taught her that at least attempting to converse in the native language went a long way towards establishing an effective relationship.

As her Audi sped through the dull landscape of northern France, she began to piece together what she knew about the men she was tracking. She had taken an instant dislike to Franklin when she'd met him at the press conference following the murder in Milton Keynes. His misogynistic behaviour had played second fiddle to his narcissism. She could see how his obvious pleasure at being there would be seen by some as indicating that he may have had something to do with what had happened. But Johnson knew better. If she were in his position, she would be doing everything to hide her actions rather than demonstrate a distinct lack of professionalism. Beyond that, there was little else she had managed to find out about him in those dark days that she'd spent in the hotel room trying to distract herself from thinking about McNeil. Franklin was never shy of providing a quote for the papers, but he had worked on few investigations that had brought about more than local attention.

Brandt, however, was entirely different. From what she could tell, he shunned the limelight and that was in spite of him having cracked a number of high profile and complex cases. Much as she hated the man who had stripped and abused her, she had to concede that he was a more than able detective. It did cause her to wonder why he had never risen beyond the post of DSI especially because, from what she imagined, any one of those successes should have put him in prime position for promotion. She didn't like to consider the fact that he may not have wanted to join the top brass because that would be too similar to her own view on career progression.

Her conclusion from all this was that it didn't make sense for Franklin to be the ringleader. She knew that her view was skewed by the fact that it was Brandt himself that had attacked her, and urged herself to remain open minded until she saw all the evidence, but this was her feeling nonetheless.

* * *

Whilst Johnson snored peacefully in her Belgian hotel room, Brandt was sat on his balcony having eventually given up on his own vain attempt to rest. The seed that had been planted on his earlier trip to the beach had germinated and was now taking root. He would kill again. As he had worked his way through the cheap, fried produce of his lunch he had attempted to resolve that it was time to put murder behind him. No longer trying to fulfil a greater purpose, he wasn't able to convince himself that the enjoyment he had derived from his actions had been a mere fortunate by-product. But as the afternoon had worn on, he found more and more ways to justify his urge. Even if it wouldn't serve to put the experience with Johnson behind him, it would give him the satisfaction of knowing that, as well as being unable to catch him, they couldn't stop him. More than that, it would give his life meaning once more. Without this he knew that, stuck in this town, his suicidal thoughts would return and the last thing he wanted to do was give them the satisfaction of finding his body washed up, with him having scaled the hill at the far side of the new town and plunged onto the rocks below. For them to believe that he had been unable to live with the guilt of his actions would be to sully the work he had done. So, he would kill, and he would keep on killing. He would manage the risk posed by limiting himself to the area in which he resided and using variety to cover his tracks. He knew that eventually the connection between the deaths would be established but, unlike before, he would work to delay that.

Content in the knowledge that the next phase of his new career would start tomorrow, Brandt headed back to bed and quickly fell into a deep and dreamless sleep.

Chapter Eighteen

Gaining the information she required was as easy as Johnson had hoped. She waited until 10am, taking a leisurely breakfast at the hotel. Although it meant more carbohydrates in the form of various pastries, given the length of time since her last decent meal, she worked her way through a number of them, washed down by plenty of excellent strong black coffee. Not only had she been correct about which police station to go to, but the officers had been very helpful there, once it had been established that it would be better for them to speak English than for her to resurrect her rusty French. It turned out that Ghent's port attracted a number of migrant workers and they were used to incidents where they were required to share information with other countries' forces. This gave cause for Johnson to work quickly, given there was every chance a real representative could arrive from England. She didn't mind that it may lead to problems for her when she returned home, as long as it didn't disrupt her investigation now.

They approached things chronologically and started by showing her the email, which she was able to decipher with relative ease. They then moved on to the paper retrieved from the car's glovebox. Johnson thought there was a good chance that, when the handwriting analysis was completed by Thames Valley, it would come back as Brandt's. She could also see why her own CID had bought into its claim that Franklin had staged the whole thing and that Brandt was a pawn in his game. Johnson was particularly impressed by how it discussed how Franklin had used leverage against Brandt but without going into specifics. If she were in a similar position to Brandt's she wouldn't want to over-egg the pudding by spending too much time talking about him. If guilt had driven Franklin to suicide, then surely it would be more about his dead victims than the man he had somehow coerced into assisting him. But whilst Brandt had been careful to suitably limit the discussion of his apparent innocence, he had failed to get Franklin to show enough of this remorse.

And this led on to the other key reason why Johnson believed it to be a work of fiction: that critical omission aside, it was too perfect. Not only was it too well written for someone who would have been in such emotional torment, but also the circumstances of it fundamentally didn't make sense. Johnson more than anyone could attest to the distance Franklin had managed to flee. Having achieved that, rather than top yourself back home, it would take some catastrophic psychological breakdown for you to end it by the edge of a lake in the middle of Belgium. But the note spoke of someone lucid and rational.

Study of the car and the body yielded no further clues, much less support for Johnson's theory that this had been the work of Brandt. The effects of sitting at the bottom of the lake for over a week was making the forensics' job a nightmare. The water was too warm for the formation of adipocere; the waxy, soapy substance that comes from fat in the body and serves to protect against decomposition. But the key damage came from the lake's wildlife. Judging by the flesh that had been removed, it must be home to some fairly large fish; ending Johnson's hopes of finding any signs that Franklin had been either bound or beaten.

She had booked a second night at the hotel in the belief that she might spend more time with the police; desperately wanting to look through CCTV from the city. But to even get them to do that themselves would require them to subscribe to the possibility that Franklin hadn't been alone. She didn't even bother trying to convince them because she knew that if her team back in Nottingham were disregarding the notion then she had little chance of making them think otherwise. So she returned to her room, via a supermarket where she picked up some supplies, to consider what she had found and plan her next steps.

She hadn't replied to the text from Claire that she had found that morning. At the time she could not work out what to say but now it simply irked her. The impatience she inferred from Claire's disingenuous inquiry into how she was, warranted a response that Johnson did not have. To tell her to leave her alone would imply she wasn't doing anything to catch her brother's killer. She didn't want that but, then again, she could hardly share what she was up to. It wasn't so much that there wasn't really anything concrete she could reveal, but more fear of what might happen in the future. Johnson knew that attempting to track down Brandt herself was a dangerous game. She hoped that, if successful, she would be able to use the authorities to catch him, but she would not run the risk of losing him again. If that meant she had to take him down herself, then that was what she was prepared to do. *Whatever it takes.* For McNeil's sake, she would accept the consequences for acting outside the law but, by the same token, she wouldn't allow his family to take on any of the culpability. Therefore, she would continue to ignore Claire and thereby keep her family in the dark until it was safe to reveal her actions.

Johnson tried to remove her thoughts from the confrontation with Brandt she so desperately craved, and to focus on the present. Even if she had it wrong and Franklin had been telling the truth in his suicide note, the fact remained Brandt had chosen to do what he did to her and McNeil. Whatever supposed leverage Franklin may have had over him, he hadn't been standing there with a gun to his head making him sexually assault her. Sometimes life presents us with hard choices and it is only then that we show our true character. Johnson didn't care there was a possibility that her overall assessment of Brandt's culpability may be wrong, she wanted him to answer for the choices he had made. Whether that was to bring him to justice in the socially acceptable and legal means, or through humanity's baser vigilantism, would just depend on how things played out.

Chapter Nineteen

Brandt was surprised how good it felt. It had been freer, and somewhat purer than before; causing any doubts as to the legitimacy of what he was doing to evaporate. Rather than undertake even a fraction of the intense planning that had gone into his deeds back home, he had woken, prepared himself a light breakfast and set out. He headed straight for the new town because he had nothing against the Spanish and wanted to target someone British. It didn't bother him that it was still quite early, and the majority of the revellers who chose this as a holiday destination would still be sleeping off their excesses from the night before; he needed relative peace if he was going to go about his business undisturbed. Moreover, it wasn't going to be holidaymakers he was targeting today. He was to kill one of the tens of thousands of ex-pats who had settled in Benidorm. Much as he disliked what Britain had become, he detested these cowards who turned their back on it. They had spent their lives in England claiming every benefit they could get their hands on, only to then sell up their ex-council house, which they had bought on the cheap in the 1980s, for a small fortune, and bugger off to another country to spend their ill-deserved proceeds there

– in someone else's economy. To top it all, they had the temerity to continue to draw their British pension. Whilst Brandt had spent his lifetime trying to make England a better, safer place, they had counted down the days until they could leave it; doing as little as possible before then. If there was one good thing to come out of Brexit it was the hope that it would stop any more of these traitors from being able to come over. If Brandt could do something to cull their numbers in the meantime, then so much the better.

He had heard about many of these people occupying large campsites on the outskirts of town. He had even seen a television programme on them once, called Bargain Loving Brits in the Sun, or some such shit, where wrinkly old UV-damaged crones boasted about how cheap they had bought their mobile home and how much better it was than being stuck in Skegness in the pouring rain. Brandt had switched over, offended; he had spent many a summer holiday in a caravan which his mother had saved bloody hard all year to afford to hire for a week. To have lazy cunts like these turn their noses up at what he had held dear to him as a child was an affront.

Much as he anticipated wreaking some havoc in these dens of the slovenly in the future, it would take more patience than he currently possessed for him to work out where they were and how to get there. It was much easier to head to the parts which he knew already, find a target, and follow them back to their abode. That they might be wealthier and own a house or apartment somewhere did not bother Brandt, for in his eyes they were all cut from the same cloth.

What he had wanted was a woman on her own. Someone young enough that it was less likely her husband had died; rather she had upped sticks and left him in the hope some young, bronzed Spanish waiter would overlook her ravaged face and saggy tits and fuck her into next week with his oily cock. Yes, he could just imagine Susan coming out here for the same reasons. What a joy it would be to bump into her in some back street or other and demonstrate that she may have been able to run but she couldn't hide.

Brandt banished dark thoughts of his ex-wife, for if he was to make sure he didn't find himself in a similar situation as he had at Johnson's house, he would need to establish that his target was really on her own rather than having gone out without her partner who remained back home. For this he would need to strike up a conversation. Much as Brandt was a solitary person, he had learned the art of putting people at ease. In many an interview of a suspect, he had successfully played the good cop to lull them into providing him with the information he required. He would do the same here and had found the perfect place in which to select his target.

Brandt had avoided the main streets in Benidorm; their proximity to the beach had led to the majority of the bars being set up there. Hence there was CCTV, to keep an eye on their patrons and their propensity for late-night trouble. Things were less guarded just a few roads back and Brandt had stumbled on a large flea market, called a *rastro* in these parts. Given the quality of the merchandise was such that he couldn't imagine a single charity shop back home failing to turn their nose up at it, the crowds there were something of a surprise. It would seem that the Brits who had moved out here weren't so much interested in finding a genuine bargain, but more spending as little of their savings as possible on essential items like clothing so they had more money for their fags and booze, and those ridiculous mobility scooters that so many of them rode around in, irrespective of not having any genuine mobility issues, other than bone idleness.

With so many people to choose from, Brandt decided to concentrate on a stall where he had the greatest chance of showing some kind of knowledge of its contents.

'They look good, them,' he said in his best East London accent, put on in case he was overheard by someone else. The fact was the tumbler was of shit quality, and Brandt had drunk many a whisky in his time.

'Do you think?' she asked pleasantly, holding it up to the light as though, like inspecting a diamond, she might somehow be able to ascertain the quality of the glass.

'May I?' he asked, reaching for its twin and performing the same bizarre routine she had. 'It's quite light really,' he commented whilst lifting it up and down in a mock drinking action. 'And that's a good thing,' he lied. 'You don't want your arm to tire and go all limp over the course of an evening.'

She laughed at his deliberately weak attempt at humour. This was a good sign; an indication that he should continue. 'Are they a present for someone? Your husband perhaps?' He kept his tone as light as possible, wanting to appear that he was just making conversation.

'Just browsing, really.' Not the response he needed so he didn't say anything in return but continued to look at her. This was a trick he had learned very early on in his career. If you wanted someone to give more detail, the best way was to allow an awkward silence to descend; they unwittingly found the need to fill it. 'I don't have a husband anymore.'

'Oh, I'm very sorry,' he replied with false solemnity.

She laughed again. 'Oh no, he's not dead or anything. I left that useless son of a bitch back in England.'

Brandt laughed too, and it was genuine. Perfect, he thought. 'Oh, you live here, do you?'

'Yes, been here two years now,' she said, having unconsciously glanced at her watch in that ridiculous way people did as though it somehow acted as a calendar. He could believe it, she had that tell-tale weathered look of a northern European complexion having had too much exposure to the sun. Not that she was unattractive. Premature aging skin aside, she was slim and had warm

134

brown eyes. Her long blonde hair was obviously an over the counter bottle job, but he bet she made more of an effort with her appearance now than she had when she'd been with her husband.

'Here in Benidorm itself?'

The second-best way to get the information you needed was to essentially repeat the same question but to sufficiently disguise it not to raise suspicion.

'Yes, I have a little house just up the road there,' she said pointing north of their position and, crucially, further away from the main part of town.

'Small world,' he stated. 'My wife and I are staying with a friend who lives a little way up there too.' It was his turn to glance at his watch. 'Oh blimey, I promised I would be back ages ago; it's just that I like to get out before the sun gets too hot, you know?'

'Oh yes, I used to feel the same when I first came out here. You soon get used to the heat, although by July and August even I start to wilt.'

Brandt joined her in laughing at this. 'Oh well, very nice to meet you,' he said turning away before facing her once again. 'I don't suppose you...?' He left the question hanging.

'What's that?' she asked, taking the bait.

'It's nothing,' he replied shaking his head. 'I was going to ask whether you wanted to walk back together, but I wouldn't want to give the wrong impression,' he continued sheepishly.

'Oh no, of course not, as long as you think your wife wouldn't mind you talking to strange women.' There was no better way to counteract the potential awkwardness of a request than being overly awkward about it.

'Ha ha, in fact I bet she would like to meet you sometime.' He started walking, sure that she would now follow. 'You see, we're considering moving out here permanently sometime and, although our friends say it's fairly easy, we would welcome another perspective. Up here, is it?' Brandt asked pointing in the same direction she had, using the question to avoid her having to respond to his suggestion they meet again, should she find it too forward.

'I'd be happy to,' she said warmly.

They chatted amiably for the remainder of their slow walk back to her place. Brandt had expected the excitement to build inside him, but he found himself considering whether he should abandon his plan. Comment about her ex-husband aside, she seemed like a nice lady and he started wondering whether he should genuinely befriend her instead. Maybe some true companionship would give his life a different meaning and she had shown every indication of enjoying his company. He was sure that he could slowly lose the accent he had put on, but abandoning other aspects of his character wouldn't be so easy. It wasn't even the fact his villa was nowhere near the direction they were heading in; he had won this woman over by his gentlemanly conduct, to then appear so willing to betray his wife would surely cause alarm and, more than likely, scare her off.

In the end, Brandt reasoned that it was much better to stick to his original plan. He tried to reassure himself that if he had found a connection with the first person he spoke to, then there was every chance, if he decided on a change of approach in the future, he would be able to find someone equally as enchanting. This time he would be conscious of there being an alternate direction for their encounter and, whilst still wanting to put them at ease, wouldn't say anything that would cause him difficulties should he decide on pursuing a relationship.

Nevertheless, out of respect for the woman who introduced herself as Julie as he pretended to bid her farewell at her door, he would keep it quick and avoid the temptation to sexually assault her despite the stirring in his groin.

'Goodbye then,' he called over his shoulder, walking away. As he slipped on his gloves, he could hear the rustling of keys and, as soon as it was accompanied by the sound of the latch opening, he began retracing his steps. She must have noticed him out of the corner of her eye because she did not enter the house but turned to give him a quizzical look.

'Tell you what, let me give you our address in case you want to pop round for a coffee sometime.' He was offering her his warmest smile, but he could see the hesitation in her eyes. But now was not the time for indecision. 'Have you got a pen and paper?' He continued, hurrying her through the door before she could begin to protest.

'Look, I'm not sure that…' She was unable to finish her sentence because Brandt's hands were suddenly round her throat, squeezing so hard that he wondered if his freshly tanned knuckles had turned white under the gloves.

'Don't fight it,' he whispered as her legs buckled underneath her.

Chapter Twenty

Johnson slept less well that night. Although she had gained the information she had come for, none of it had put her mind at rest. There just seemed nothing to go on and if she were in that situation in her own CID, she would be able to have the team keep working over the evidence until something was revealed. But that wasn't an option here, so she started packing up, ready to make the long journey back home again. Much as she was frustrated to be leaving without a trail to follow, it was with more irritation that she found she was unable to book herself on a Channel Tunnel train until late in the evening, having originally foregone the additional cost of buying an open ticket.

With the mandatory checkout time looming, she left her car parked at the hotel and took a walk into town to kill a couple of hours. She may have resented being there, but she had to admit the centre of Ghent was attractive with its medieval buildings. Heading towards Gravensteen Castle, as that seemed the main attraction for the small amount of tourism the area received, Johnson stopped off for a coffee on her way. Given her efforts to practice her French had lasted a mere sentence at the police station, she welcomed another opportunity to try the local language.

However, the simple process of ordering a coffee and a cake had been a challenge for Johnson, given the scowl provided by the waitress before silently going to prepare her items. With the distinct lack of a warm welcome, Johnson didn't linger longer than it took to consume her snack and, without even a glance in the waitress' direction, she counted out the exact change and continued on her journey.

The castle itself was attractive enough and certainly grander than those she had visited in Britain but, after spending a few minutes wandering the battlements and admiring the views, she soon became bored and headed back to her car, lying to herself that she would drive slower than before; more realistically surmising that arriving at the terminal may see her squeezed onto an earlier train. Perhaps flashing her warrant card could aid the process if she implied she was returning from police business which, technically, she was. Suspicious that the refreshments offered at Calais might be a bit more geared towards French tastes than they had been at Folkestone, she decided she would pick up a filled baguette at one of the delicatessens she had passed before. Johnson was still full from breakfast, not to mention her brief café stop, but nibbling on it may help to combat the boredom of the journey that lay ahead.

She entered the shop trying to recall whether it was un or une baguette and decided to stick to the more familiar fillings she could remember of jambon, poulet or fromage et salade. It wasn't so much that the young man decided to respond in his basic English, delivered in his thick accent, but more his exasperated tone that irked Johnson.

'Is there a problem with my French?'

'English is better, no?' he replied slowly, clearly trying to work out the words in his mind as he went.

'No offence but I think my French is better than your English.' She tried to add a smile at the end to soften the criticism.

'My English not good; my French more not good.'

'Excuse me?' Johnson was lost now.

He sighed. 'My English okay. My French bad.'

'Your French is bad but you're Belgian, aren't you?' Johnson was shocked. Why would you employ someone who couldn't speak the language? Even before she witnessed the offence in the man's expression, she realised the mistake she had made. 'You're Flemish, aren't you?'

He replied in a language Johnson didn't know but sounded to her like Dutch.

'I'm really sorry,' she replied honestly.

'Is okay,' he shrugged. 'Many English do same.'

'But it's culturally insensitive.'

'I not know these words,' he replied, shaking his head.

With Johnson unable to explain that she now understood why speaking French to people living in the Flanders region of Belgium was wrong, she completed her order as quickly as possible. It didn't stop her wondering what they did when actual French people visited the region, but she supposed it wasn't so offensive when they were speaking their own language rather than assuming all Belgians were essentially French. She was also put in mind of her infrequent visits to Wales where she had always wondered the point of going to the effort of having all road signs in Welsh as well as English, given that everyone in Wales spoke English. She accepted now that it was less about linguistic ability and more cultural identity.

Nevertheless, given how she was feeling that morning, she left the shop thinking she could have done without the lesson provided for her by the young man. She turned in the direction of the hotel and stopped suddenly. Perhaps the timing was more fortuitous than she realised. She rushed back to her car replaying the conversation she'd had with the detective when she first arrived at the station yesterday. She hadn't picked up any kind of offence but, now she thought of it, his keenness to switch to English might not have been due to her rusty attempt at speaking French.

He seemed genuinely surprised to see her again, not helped by the fact it appeared she had only returned to apologise for failing to realise he was Flemish.

'Truly, it's not a problem,' he said, trying to reassure her. 'We get that all the time.'

'But the locals all speak Flemish,' she responded hurriedly.

'Yes, I know they can be a little, er… how you say, awkward. Just forget it.'

'No, you don't understand. The email was in French!'

The detective's casual and easy-going nature, which had been useful yesterday, was now a source of annoyance for Johnson. He didn't seem too fazed that a local would write in French and explained that they had checked the IP address and it came from Ghent. His response to her suggestion that it was too odd to ignore was met with a shrug that she would have described as Gallic, had it not been for what she had recently discovered.

It had taken quite a bit of convincing to get him to agree to take them around to the address associated with the sending of the email but, once in the car, which she noted was a German Mercedes, rather than a French Peugeot, Renault or Citroen, he relaxed again. The sat nav guided them to a property on the outskirts of town, where an elderly gentlemen lived on his own. Whilst the detective spoke to him in Flemish, Johnson wondered whether he even owned a computer, but heard the word Skype a couple of times and didn't need the translation that followed to understand that he had the internet so he could keep in touch with his grown-up children. The man confirmed that, as far as he was aware, no one else had used his computer recently nor, more significantly, had he been to the lake.

With the detective seemingly satisfied with what he had heard, despite confiding to her in English that he expected nothing less considering the author of the email had clearly wanted to remain anonymous, Johnson turned to the man. 'Habitez-vous ici longtemps?' she asked, putting on her very best accent.

All Johnson received in response was a blank look.

Chapter Twenty-one

Brandt's lasting impression from the day before was one of hope. The regret he felt at having to kill Julie had been brief and he instead concentrated on what his meeting with her had taught him. Benidorm was still a bit crass for his tastes, but he believed that, with the right person, he could become settled there; perhaps even happy. He wasted little time in coming up with his next plan. Even though a little research taught him there were many rastros similar to the market he had visited yesterday, a change of scenery would be sensible given what had happened. And yet the role of the newly arrived Brit, looking to explore the viability of moving out there long term, remained suitable, so he settled on visiting an auction house on the outskirts of town. From its basic website, clearly created by someone who had very little experience with IT, he saw that it was owned by an ex-pat and, from what he could gather, was frequented by his fellow countrymen.

With the summer heat having already built to near intolerable levels by mid-morning, Brandt took a taxi rather than walk the mile or two there. Given his motivation for meeting someone was different to previous encounters, he didn't feel the need to cover his tracks but didn't call for the car to meet him at his villa; instead electing a little café down the road.

The plain-looking warehouse seemed perfect and was already busy with people checking out the items for sale prior to the start of the auction. He began looking around, marvelling at the amount of interest the cheap tat on display seemed to be generating. None of it held even remote appeal to Brandt but he worked his way across the room, pausing occasionally to study one item or another. After a few minutes of doing this, and to avoid seeming too proficient, he put on a puzzled expression and became more haphazard with his search for goods to bid on.

This new approach must have worked, because almost immediately a woman came up to him. 'It can be a bit daunting at first,' she said.

He turned around to offer her a confused smile, taking in her dark tan that matched her brown hair and eyes. 'Er yes, there's so much to look through.'

'It's like this every time. It'll all sell though, and next week there'll be another load of stuff.'

'Where does it all come from?' Brandt asked, enjoying small talk for one of the very few occasions in his life.

'Well, mostly house clearances, you see. There's a number of guys who spend the week buying up items from people who are upgrading or just looking to move on. It's mostly their stuff here and Gary, who owns this place, takes a cut from everything sold.'

'Sounds like you come here often.'

'Pretty much every week for the last two years. When I first moved out,' Brandt noticed she spoke in the singular, 'I came here to furnish my place but when I had done that, I just kept on coming.'

'Why was that?' He was genuinely intrigued. It was a hot day and, if he wasn't here for a specific purpose, there were few places he could think of worse to spend time in.

'I suppose I hate the idea that I might miss out on a bargain and, anyway, there's the social side.' Smiling, she regarded his raised eyebrow. 'You tend to meet the same people up here every week but there's always the new fish who help to keep things fresh.'

Brandt considered what he had learned so far. He guessed that she was somewhere in her mid 50s but, effects of her tan aside, could probably pass for younger. Although he had come to consider himself more of a gentleman who preferred blondes, she suited her dark features. Everything she had said suggested she was single but liked meeting new people. So, all in all, very promising and, it would seem that his meeting of Julie yesterday hadn't just been beginner's luck.

'David,' he said offering her his hand.

She gave a childish giggle at his formality. 'Trish,' she replied. 'So, what brings you here, David?'

'Well, I'm just looking really. You see, I'm currently considering moving out here permanently and am trying to decide whether to take the plunge and buy something outright or just rent for a while. If I do rent, it's worth knowing if I should pay the extra for a furnished apartment or whether it would be better to pick up my own items.'

'Oh, definitely worth getting your own,' she replied animatedly. 'There's always some good stuff here and it's dirt cheap compared to what you'd pay back home. Listen,' she leaned in closer. 'Take my advice and don't over think it. Just take the plunge and move out here. You can feel your way as you go.'

'Is that what you did?'

'Yep, spur of the moment. I bought a caravan online and flew out the next day. Never looked back.'

'You just went ahead and bought it?' Brandt could tell she was proud of her impetuousness and he wanted to allow her to string out her sharing of her experience.

'Yep, no photos, just transferred over my €4,000 and booked my flight. Had a bit of a fright when I got here, mind, the previous owner hadn't got around to telling the

145

campsite manager yet, and he didn't have a clue who I was! Thought for a moment I had been scammed or something. Turned out alright in the end though.'

'Wow, that's quite a story,' he exaggerated. 'I'm not sure I'm brave enough to do that.'

'If there's one thing I've learned in life,' she said, placing a reassuring hand on his arm. 'Is that you regret the things you don't do, more than the things you do.'

He nodded in a manner he hoped looked sagely. 'Very true. Are you still there now?'

'Oh yes, absolutely!' She beamed. 'It was only meant to be a stop gap until I found a villa but once I did it up and added my own personal touch, I couldn't stand to leave it. Plus, the atmosphere at the campsite is amazing. Everyone is so welcoming, it's a lovely little community there. Have you considered buying a caravan?'

'Well I er...'

'Ah come on, Mr Snobby,' she said, not unkindly. 'Look I felt the same but, honestly, it's nothing like what you expect from back home.' She paused, offering him a broad smile. 'Tell you what, why don't I show you around when we've finished up here?'

'I'd like that,' he replied, meaning it. In the same way he had begun to revise his overall impression of Benidorm, perhaps his preconception of what the caravan sites would be like may also be wrong. Anyway, he welcomed the chance to spend a little more time in the company of Trish. She seemed friendly enough and he liked the way she hadn't asked him any personal questions. Nevertheless, he didn't want to seem too keen, so he excused himself and found a seat ready for the start of the auction.

His initial interest in the swift delivery of Gary the auctioneer, and the pittance the items seemed to be sold for, quickly waned. If it had not been for Trish's promise, Brandt would have discreetly made his exit long before the end. But when it was finally over, and the people started moving around to depart or to settle up for items they had purchased, he couldn't spot her anywhere. Not usually very proficient in social situations, he started to wonder whether her offer had just been part of the small talk and disingenuous. But, as he stepped outside in the hope that he may find a taxi waiting rather than having to call for one, he spotted her smoking just off to the right. The relief he felt outweighed his revulsion at her foul habit.

Brandt didn't have to consider whether it would be appropriate to approach her because she immediately noticed him and offered an enthusiastic wave. 'Oh, there you are, I was beginning to think I'd lost you,' she called across.

He smiled, unsure how to respond.

'My car's just over here,' she gestured. 'If you still want the grand tour that is.'

He walked over and followed her to an old Seat Ibiza, whose dark blue paint had a mottled appearance. The stale smell of tobacco inside suggested that her decision to toss the remains of her cigarette before getting in was out of courtesy to him rather than any sort of care for the maintenance of her vehicle.

This impression was confirmed by her somewhat erratic driving style. The journey passed pleasantly enough for Brandt though, enjoying as he did the cooling effects of the wind rushing through his open window and the effortless conversation dominated by Trish.

He was similarly impressed by the sight that greeted him as they pulled into the caravan park. 'It looks massive,' he commented.

'Sure is,' she replied amiably. 'There's a number of these sites around Benidorm but this is the largest.' To emphasise the point, she proceeded to drive to the top of the first road, so he could see how many similar rows stretched out to his left. Taking the next one back down, she parked near the entertainment centre at the front. 'Thirsty work,' she said, clearly having noticed the longing look he offered the bar area. 'Let's go and take a look at the pool first, shall we?'

'You're the boss,' he said, getting out of the car and regretting no longer being able to feel the rush of cooling air on his skin. He had barely a chance to admire the way the well-established trees provided a natural boundary, along with welcome shade between the pitches, when they arrived at the communal pool. It was as good as any he had seen, and he admired the way the grass surrounding it was lush and green.

'A proper little oasis here,' he said before looking around. 'It's a bit quiet though isn't it?'

Trish laughed. 'I can tell you're new to Spanish living. Most people go back to their homes for a siesta in the height of the day.'

'But...'

'I know what you're thinking. All that metal and the effects of the sun? Well, most of us have air conditioning but those of us who have acclimatised tend to lie out under our awnings. Come, let me show you.' Before he could respond, she grabbed his arm and led him into another of the park's many lanes.

In isolation the caravans themselves were far less impressive than the large static ones that dominated the sites back home, but it was what the residents had added that set them miles apart. What Trish had described as an awning didn't do justice to the complex structures added as an extension to the small mobile homes. There were gardens too, often with exotic plants and flowers, and most places had their own small fencing surrounding their space. Brandt was starting to understand why Trish had decided to remain here, rather than go for one of the impersonal apartments closer to the town centre.

'Here we are,' she said as they arrived outside a particularly attractive plot. If she hadn't told him what she had paid for the caravan itself, he would scarcely have believed you could get a place like this so cheap. 'It took

148

me nearly a year to get it how I wanted it,' she said modestly, leading him through the gate and into a square room constructed out of canvas. It contained a large corner-style sofa with a throw and pink cushions scattered over it. Already it seemed nicer than the brief look he had at Julie's house the day before. 'In the summer I tend to sleep out here rather than the smaller accommodation inside, but I can see you're suffering a bit from the heat so let's go into the kitchen and I can get the air con cranked up.'

'Too early for a gin, is it?' Trish asked as soon as Brandt had followed her inside.

Whisky may have been his spirit of choice but at that moment he could think of nothing he would like more. 'Absolutely not,' he said confidently, taking a seat in the small lounge area. He adjusted his position to be more in line with the cold air which had already started pumping through. As Trish rummaged round the cupboards before going into the fridge to collect the tonic water, Brandt couldn't help but feel he had landed on his feet. It had never been his intention to leave Britain, much less to come to somewhere like Benidorm. And yet he had managed to turn what should have been a very negative situation, with how things had transpired in Nottingham, to his advantage. As Trish approached him, condensation forming on the glasses she held in each hand, and her light summer dress sashaying with her movement, he allowed himself a smug smile.

Taking a long swig of the cool liquid and savouring the generous ratio of spirit to mixer, he didn't notice that Trish had not only failed to sit but had also placed down her glass; its contents untouched. As he finally looked up, he didn't have time to register the sound of her hands opening the zip at the back of her dress before it fell to the floor. He was shocked by the sight of her stood before him in just her white knickers; a stark contrast to the dark hue of her skin. This was the first time he had even considered her breasts but given how pert and youthful they looked, on reflection, he was not surprised that she hadn't seen the need to wear a bra.

'Like what you see?' she asked, lifting her fingers to pinch her nipples; an action that saw them immediately stiffen. 'I paid a lot more for these than I did for this place.' The confidence she exuded in sharing the fact she'd had cosmetic surgery was reflected in the way she regarded Brandt. 'You look a little surprised?' Her tone was playful but bordered on mocking.

The truth was Brandt was stunned. He had expected nothing like this. When she had invited him in, it hadn't even remotely crossed his mind that she was doing anything more than extending the tour she had offered him. But Trish didn't wait for a response. She slowly sunk to her knees and expertly unbuttoned his shorts and unzipped the fly. He had barely processed what was about to happen when her mouth was enveloping him. The sensation was pleasant but counteracted by thoughts of how they had got to this stage. He considered the various comments he had made, trying to see how any of them could have been misconstrued as suggestive. But whilst he couldn't find any specific examples, he did wonder whether the apparent ease of their conversation had hidden her true intention all along. Brandt hadn't wanted this, he had sought companionship to combat the deep loneliness he was feeling in an unfamiliar town in an alien country; not to be used and no doubt discarded when he had served his purpose.

He looked down to see her working away on him energetically, suddenly embarrassed at his inability to find the required physical response to her attention. As she suddenly sat up and his penis flopped back onto his testicles, he feared the worse. 'There's no rush,' she whispered soothingly, standing up and then slipping off her knickers. She stood before him, his head at the perfect position to take in what had been revealed. Aside from a faint scar he assumed to be from a long-ago caesarean section, her skin was as near flawless as her stomach was flat. The way she waited patiently whilst he regarded her perfectly trimmed pubic hair suggested a total comfort in her own appearance. But what she didn't know was that, rather than stimulate Brandt, it only heightened his anxiety. For her to demonstrate such care in her appearance, especially in an area so private and that could only have been shaved as recently as this morning, added to the feeling that he was merely being used. What she had said about going to the auction to meet people he realised had hidden a deeper truth where she used it to feed her sex addiction. A voice in his head spoke out to suggest that, even if it were the case, he should be flattered that someone as particular as her should select him, but an even louder one told him she would soon realise her faith had been misplaced if he continued not to perform.

Desperate to prove it wrong he pushed Trish back so that she stumbled into the bench seating facing him and slumped down. Before she could open her mouth to protest, he opened her legs, pushed his face into the gap he had created and performed an act unknown to him for two decades. Nevertheless, the taste and her moans of pleasure, steadily increasing in both frequency and volume, convinced him it was a skill well remembered.

He became sure that when the inevitable orgasm came, he would gain the confidence to accept that whether it took a long time, or indeed transpired to be far quicker than he would have ideally have liked, he would feel worthy of being intimate with her. But just as he started to feel himself relax into the situation, she grabbed his head and pulled him away from her. 'I want to come with you inside me,' she panted, sitting up. Her cheeks were flushed but the glassy look in her eyes cleared as she glanced down at his still flaccid penis. She was unable to hide her disappointment.

The shame that Brandt had expected to feel didn't wash over him. Instead he was angry. It was symptomatic of the arrogance of this woman that she would expect his pleasuring of her to provide the impetus her attention on him had failed to achieve. Her earlier words of there being no rush were clearly a lie. She wanted him to get on with it, so they could finish, and she could kick him out of her caravan and out of her life before the ice in her gin and tonic had melted.

'Is this the first time since…'

'Since?' he asked, his voice low and menacing.

'Since your wife…'

He failed to notice the concern and compassion in her voice, such was the rage that overwhelmed him at the mere mention of that bitch in this context. His arms thrust out before him and immediately grabbed her throat. This time he didn't need to wonder whether he was exerting enough pressure to change the colour of his knuckles; he could see them himself. But that was nothing compared to the alarming shade of Trish's face. With her supply of air choked off, and her arms flailing in a futile attempt to force him to release his grip, she was turning purple and her eyes were bulging in their sockets. But rather than become horrified at his destruction of her natural beauty, Brandt could finally feel himself stiffen.

Chapter Twenty-two

Johnson made it to Calais in time for her own booking. If anything, the revelation made staying in Ghent more pointless. If, as she suspected, the email was from Brandt, it was part of his effort to conceal his real destination. She had no idea where it was, but one thing was for certain – it wasn't Belgium.

But Johnson had a bigger problem: even if she could work out where he had gone after faking Franklin's suicide, the question remained what she would do with that knowledge. Without the resources she enjoyed as a police officer, even if she was lucky enough to establish which town he was in, it would leave her far from actually catching him. The logical solution would be to pass that information on to the authorities but doing that wouldn't be as simple as it sounded. First would be the question as to how she had come to know this. Even if she could convince Potter that she had done nothing improper, there was also the issue of whether they would actually believe her. She could imagine the conversation where she tried to explain that an email sent in French in the Flanders region of Belgium indicated someone covering their tracks. They were sure to laugh her out of the station. Nevertheless, chief among her concerns was that the police would mess it up and Brandt would escape again. It was hard for her to admit such a thing, having devoted much of her adult life to the force, and making many sacrifices along the way but, much as she despised Brandt, she knew he was a strong adversary. He was more aware of their investigative methods than they were, and even gaining a sniff of a police presence might see him disappear altogether. The fact remained that it was only when Johnson acted outside of police protocol with her unsolicited discussion with the columnist, Gail Trevelly, that he had surfaced. Moreover, he had done a good job of convincing everyone not only that he'd remained in the country but also that, despite being the one to attack her and kill McNeil, he was somehow just a pawn in someone else's game.

Johnson could feel the anger rising inside and calmed herself by thinking that all this was academic unless she could figure out where Brandt had gone. As she made her way around the M25, which she found surprisingly busy given how late at night it now was, she tried to focus on what she did know. The purpose of the email was obvious: he was ready for Franklin's body to be found. He had initially concealed it to enable a successful getaway and, a week later, people's memory of anything out of the ordinary would have faded to the extent of making it useless. He wanted Franklin's body to be found so that it corroborated the impression they had parted as soon as things went wrong in Nottingham. This would also explain why he'd gone to such efforts to conceal his identity. The disguising of IP addresses was no small feat, and certainly something Johnson didn't know how to do, and she made a mental note of him either being proficient in computing or having the wherewithal to successfully research his IT needs.

But Johnson couldn't help thinking this all had the whiff of overkill. If Franklin's suicide note was as carefully scripted as she believed it to be, then she wondered as to the true purpose of it. Brandt would know that the manhunt would continue even if it was felt his role was lesser than had first appeared. Therefore, it made no sense for its primary objective to be to absolve himself of some of the responsibility. Given he had actively sought to provide the police the links between the initial attacks, it seemed counter-intuitive. Johnson knew this was something she would need to think on further, but it certainly suggested to her an element of ego. Even if it hadn't been for her successful goading of him regarding his sexuality, his efforts to cover up whatever he had seen as going wrong in St. Albans with the attack on Lily James, suggested he wanted his actions to be viewed in a very specific way.

There was no doubt in her mind that, even if she had retained the resources available to her as a detective, he remained by far the most complex character she had investigated. Given what he had done to her personally, anyone would forgive Johnson for having such a narrow-minded view of Brandt, but she would not allow herself to fail to appreciate the qualities she would need to overcome if she was to catch him. That he knew the intimate workings of the police force was now a given, but acceptance of that would also be to disregard his general high level of intelligence. Take his use of French, for instance. Whilst Johnson was able to read what he had written, she would have no hope of constructing such perfect sentences herself.

She swerved violently in the road, causing the car in the middle lane to have to take evasive action to avoid her hitting him. The blast of his horn served to restore her senses and she eased back on the throttle, pulled into the left-hand lane and set the Audi's cruise control at a sedate 70mph. Johnson had realised her mistake. In her effort to not allow her personal emotions to cloud her analysis of the evidence presented to her, she had gone too far the other way and was giving Brandt more credit than he deserved. She had been right; his French was perfect. Too perfect. Someone with the ability to divert their IP address to another country would have no problems with something as simple as Google Translate. She knew from her time studying French that, a bit like in the game of Chinese whispers, when you converted text into another language and translated it back into its original form, it changed slightly. Not by a huge amount, but every dialect had its own idiosyncrasies. If one machine literally translated them, it altered the language to the extent that to change it back would see you with a different sentence to the original.

Johnson knew that she required more confirmation of Brandt's linguistic skills than feeding it back through Google Translate. He had been careful to keep his phrases short to avoid making any obvious mistakes, and she was sure she wouldn't be wise to it now had it not been for her accidental discovery of him using the wrong language for the particular region he was claiming to be from. But none of this meant he didn't know any French, or in fact any other languages that he could rely on when trying to settle in a different country. She would need to find out the level of his ability because, if it transpired he had none, then that could massively narrow down her search area for him. She was convinced that his fleeing abroad had never been part of the plan, and she would put money on it being an opportunistic decision to use Franklin in that way. Therefore, if he found himself in continental Europe on a hastily conceived escape, unable to speak any of the native languages, it would see him seek out places where he could rely on speaking English without arousing suspicion.

As Johnson exited the M1 at Junction 25 and followed the A52 towards Nottingham, she did not turn off onto the road that would lead to her flat. Instead she continued on towards the police station where she hoped to God none of the team had decided to work deep into the night.

The car park was pleasingly quiet as she pulled in. Johnson knew that Sergeant Andrews tended to work the day shift but, all the same, was relieved to find a different person stood at the duty desk. She didn't even recognise her, let alone know her name, but the nod she gave Johnson suggested she knew exactly who she was, and Johnson would just have to hope that she either wasn't aware of her supposed holiday leave or didn't view her arrival at the station as sufficiently strange to want to comment on it to someone in the morning.

The CID floor appeared to be empty but the lights still being on caused Johnson to enter with caution. With no one in the main area, she believed herself to be alone and wandered in the direction of her office. The sight of Potter's door opening caused a yelp of fright to escape, and her mind immediately began thinking of possible excuses for her being there; all of which she immediately dismissed as preposterous.

'I'm sorry to frighten you, miss,' replied the middle-aged woman pulling a vacuum cleaner behind her.

Johnson's barely concealed relief was such that she had to resist hugging her. 'That's not a problem,' she mumbled uncomfortably, before striding to her office. Certain that her nerves could not take any further surprises, she wasted no time in logging on and retrieving the details she required. Having noted down the phone number and address of Mrs Susan Brandt, she also added the same for Franklin's wife just in case she needed that information in the future.

Offering the cleaner an unreciprocated wave of farewell, she went back down the stairs and was pleased to find the duty sergeant busy dealing with a drunk and disorderly trying to talk his way out of whatever charges she was reading to him.

Johnson's apprehension at having to introduce herself to the wife of the man who had attacked her, was outweighed by her desire to get the information she

157

craved. However, stood in the car park and observing the stars in the clear night sky, she knew that she was far more likely to find the woman cooperative if she wasn't waking her in the early hours of the morning. Instead she drove slowly back to her flat listening to some late-night music on the radio she didn't recognise but found herself tapping along to on the steering wheel. With the weariness of her travels finally catching up with her, she forewent the shower she had promised herself on the long journey back from Folkestone, but did have one final job to do before she would allow herself to collapse into her, still unfamiliar, bed.

Chapter Twenty-three

Brandt woke up late with the oppression of a heavy hangover clouding his immediate thoughts. This was the first time he had drank to such excess since arriving in Benidorm, and it took him a few moments to establish the root cause of his over-indulgence the day before. If the heat that had steadily built up in the room over the course of the morning hadn't been enough to see him already sweating, remembering what he had done would have provoked the same physical reaction. It wasn't so much the fact that he had been compelled to kill again, nor even the circumstances that had led to his actions, but the manner in which it had been done that caused him alarm. He had let his guard down in so many ways yesterday and there was every chance that poor decision would come back to haunt him.

Selecting an auction house rather than a market was his first mistake. He had gone out of town which meant there was a more captive audience than the casual footfall of a rastro. He hadn't seen any CCTV cameras there but, then again, he hadn't been specifically looking. Trish had even said to him that she visited there every week so it wouldn't take very long at all for them to be able to retrace her steps. Anyone who had seen her talking to Brandt at the auction would be able to narrow down the possible suspects to the new guy, even in the unlikely situation they couldn't provide much of a description. A quick ring around the taxi companies would soon reveal his approximate location.

But there was one simple fact that made all the other mistakes pale into insignificance. His identity would be all over the crime scene. As soon as she died, and was lying in the puddle of her own urine, he had wiped his glass and anywhere else he believed he may have come into contact with. But even at the time he had known it was an effort in futility. Having not worn his gloves, there would be many places he couldn't remember touching, not least on Trish's actual body. Even in the unlikely event that he had removed all his prints, there was his DNA. There shouldn't be any of his blood but almost certainly there would be some of his hairs and there would definitely be his saliva on her. It wasn't standard practice for the police to run their tests against databases in other countries but given the victim was an ex-pat, and the murder took place in a caravan site full of Brits, they would be stupid not to share the DNA with the UK police force. Brandt would be immediately identified and, given his history, a manhunt on a massive scale would be undertaken.

The only sensible thing to do was to escape now, for he had already wasted many precious hours. But it wasn't just the debilitating effects of his hangover that was causing him to be reluctant. He resented the fact that some old slag was driving him from the place he was trying his best to make home. He didn't regret killing her; she thoroughly deserved it for her deceptive and predatory ways. Naturally he knew that he would be in a far better position now if she were not dead, but sometimes people had to reap what they had sown. His hesitation was fear of rushing his escape and making a mistake. He had managed to improvise successfully after the events in Nottingham but careful, well thought out planning beat blind panic every time. The fact of the matter was he didn't know where he should flee. The notion of going somewhere with plenty of English-speaking people was a sound one and, with it being the summer months, there would be many such places to choose from. But the police would be expecting him to do this because his original selection of Benidorm more than hinted at a desire to be among his own people. As a consequence, the obvious places that sprung to mind along the Costa Blanca and Costa del Sol would also occur to them. No longer having the advantage of his new look and them believing he was still in Britain, would mean the likelihood of him remaining undetected would be slim at best.

Therefore, the worst thing he could do was unnecessarily rush his departure. He needed to allow himself time to find somewhere suitable to go to and the means to get there. Maybe even create a diversion by leaving a false trail. Perhaps he could go to the bus station and buy himself a ticket somewhere. He knew from experience how to tread the fine line between making it too subtle that he wouldn't be picked up on CCTV, and too obvious where a decent detective would smell a rat. To help he would need to make his villa look like he'd left in a hurry. Leaving his laptop would certainly give that impression and there was nothing on it which, by that stage, they wouldn't already know about. Moreover, he could add to his search history destinations that corroborated the false ticket he bought.

Already Brandt could feel his mood lift. He wouldn't let that whore from yesterday pull him down; he was determined to turn a negative into a positive. The key thing in all this was how much time he had. The only way he could get a suitable indication was to find out whether her body had been discovered. Given that he would use his time online to also research his next true destination, he knew that heading to the internet café just as soon as he'd taken a shower and put on some clean clothes was the best idea.

Whereas there had been times in Britain where he had been paranoid of having been discovered, to the extent where he had sat at home one night ready to slash his own throat, he felt remarkably calm as he took the walk into the centre of Benidorm. That the owner of the internet café recognised Brandt from his previous visit wasn't a worry because, again, he found something to busy himself with at the other end of the room, leaving him in peace. Nevertheless, Brandt did feel nervous as he accessed the local newsfeed; his fears realised by a story from yesterday evening about the discovery of a woman strangled in her home. The urge to just run, there and then, was strong but he found himself clicking onto the article itself. The surge of relief that swept through him was palpable when he read that it was referring to the woman from the market. With more recent events at the forefront of his mind he had almost forgotten about his encounter with Julie, and he allowed himself the pleasure of reading about his exploits before switching back to the news feed. There was nothing about Trish. Having read how a friend of Julie's had become suspicious when she had failed to meet with him that evening, Brandt had been sure that one of Trish's many fuck buddies would have gone around to her sordid den of iniquity last night and discovered her. It would seem even serial sex perverts like her sometimes took the night off.

Brandt relaxed in his seat. He figured there would be six hours as an absolute minimum between the body's discovery and it being traced back to his villa. And for that to happen, everything would have to work out seamlessly. The forensics would have to do their job quickly and efficiently. The local police would have to make the call to share the findings with the UK as soon as the results came back. They would then have to retrace her steps to the auction and establish that she had been talking to a stranger, before focusing on the taxi companies. Having figured out where Brandt had hailed his cab, they would need to work door to door to find where he had been staying. Six hours as an absolute minimum and likely much, much longer. He also knew he would be aware when the timer started. In these days of social media, it didn't pay for the police to delay breaking the news of an incident. People instantly posting pictures of the cordoned off areas and speculating as to what had happened needed to be addressed before sensationalism and panic set in.

Brandt was going to head back to the villa to get himself some lunch. It wasn't complacency because he could use the time to think about possible destinations before cracking on that afternoon with the real research. Just before logging off, he had a quick check of his emails. He wasn't going to because of the hassle of rerouting the IP address but he was interested to see whether the Belgian police had sent any form of reply. He wasn't surprised when the main page announced he had an unread email because, if not from them, it was likely to be yet another welcome message for his new account advertising some feature or other he had no interest in.

– *I KNOW WHO YOU ARE.*

Just the subject line; no text in the main body and from an email address that was just a random selection of letters and numbers.

Brandt's blood ran cold. He was unable to stop himself glancing around the room to see if he was being watched at that very moment. He needed to get out of there, not for lunch, but for fear that the very person who had written this could somehow now see him through his computer.

He not so much as walked out of the internet café, more staggered, and unconsciously made his way down to the beach before collapsing in a sun lounger. There must have been something about the way he looked because the

163

attendant, who initially approached to charge him for the rental, suddenly backed away again.

So many questions were flooding Brandt's mind. Who? How? Why? He lay there wondering whether the tightening he could feel in his chest was the result of an impending heart attack. What an inauspicious way to go that would be. But slowly and steadily he could feel his pulse lessen and his mind gain some clarity of thought. For sure this was an unexpected and unwelcome development but, in the context of things, what did it truly matter? As soon as Trish's body was discovered they would know that he must have left the country with Franklin and therefore the events at the lake in Ghent would also have something to do with him. As a consequence, it wouldn't be a stretch of the imagination to assume that he had orchestrated the discovery of the body too. But whilst Brandt could accept that his actions yesterday – albeit having been forced into them by the devious old slapper – would lead to this, it disturbed him to think that someone was already steps ahead of him. It reminded him of Franklin's revelation that the police already had an image of him near the crime scenes but, this time, far worse.

He forced himself to go to a nearby bar and order some food. He hadn't eaten since early yesterday and would need the energy if he was going to make his escape this afternoon. Whilst ordering his all-day breakfast, he also selected a beer, reasoning it might help to settle his nerves and, if not, a hair of the dog may combat his still-present hangover. One lager turned into three and he had to fight the impulse to bury his concerns in the sweet oblivion promised by inebriation. The mild buzz he was getting from the relatively small amount of alcohol in his system allowed him to evaluate the email with more rationality than before. Somehow someone had realised it was he who had sent the email informing the Belgian police of Franklin's whereabouts. That was it. Brandt was relieved that he had made sure that its origin would remain hidden. Naturally, his mysterious pen friend might be hiding further information they had uncovered but if the purpose of the message, as would seem apparent, was to unsettle him, why hold back? There was a certain arrogance to the claim they knew who he was, and it surely suggested that, if they knew more, they would choose to reveal that too and increase the pressure. It was highly unlikely that this was the work of the police because it would be counter-intuitive for them to try and spook him. They liked to lull their quarry into a false sense of security so that when they finally did pounce, it was unexpected.

The number of people with the motive to send such a thing was unfathomable. The purpose of Brandt's actions had been to awaken society from their slumber of indifference and there would be plenty of nut jobs out there who would love to track him down. Yet the number of those with the means to even be aware of the email he had sent the Belgian police, let alone find out the address he had used, was small. But there was no point dwelling on this for now; his limited time would be far better spent planning his escape along with setting up the false trail. For the moment, he would just have to take the risk and work on the assumption that this person wasn't aware of his current location, rather than rush his preparations.

His afternoon spent back at the internet café proved to be useful. There had been no further emails and nor had there been any news of Trish's murder. Still unsure as to the best place to head, he focused instead on the false trail. Unsure whether a passport would be required to get to one of the Balearic Islands, he finally settled on Torremolinos. It was the first of the Costa del Sol tourist resorts and, by all accounts, still a popular holiday destination for the British. It made sense to Brandt that someone who chose Benidorm would then select this place as the next best option. That it was a long way down the coast would assist in making it not seem too obvious, but the only thing that troubled Brandt was that there were no direct bus or coach routes. Clearly, he couldn't buy a plane ticket without a passport, and the train would be similarly pointless because it wouldn't take long to use the network's CCTV cameras to establish that he had never used his ticket. Instead he would buy a bus pass to Malaga and use his laptop back at the villa to give the impression he was using that as his first stop on the way to Torremolinos. That there would be no further evidence of his travelling there didn't concern him too much. It made sense for someone fleeing in a hurry to take the chance of purchasing a ticket at the bus station, only to work more covertly by hitchhiking or taking a more indirect route once they were clear of the immediate danger.

By the time Brandt had first gone home to complete his fake research, and then to the bus station to purchase an open ticket to Malaga – needing to do it in that order to ensure the chronology of his actions was consistent – he was wired and thought a visit to a bar before retiring for the night would be wise. His lunchtime pints had given him a taste for beer that had remained with him throughout the afternoon and he reasoned that this may be the last time he could afford to be in such a public place for a while. After a swift return to the internet café to check that the body was still undiscovered, he settled on one of the various show bars in the new town. Selecting a discreet table in the corner to avoid the sort of attention that had landed him in so much trouble yesterday, he steadily worked his way through a few drinks and found the entertainment to be far better than the free entry suggested it might. Top billing was a drag act and, although Brandt was a traditionalist and tended to shy away from anything he considered deviant, he found himself laughing at the bawdy humour and clapping along to her various musical numbers.

Pottering home afterwards, and resisting the urge to simply move on to one of the other all-night bars, Brandt felt a tremendous sadness to think that this was probably his last night in Benidorm. His early impressions of its crassness remained true, but he had found a certain synergy with the place and regretted that there would be no more evenings like this. Even his villa had started to feel like home and, as he shut his front door, he sought to embrace his melancholy as a sign that he was not done with life yet. Absolutely, he had suffered yet another setback but whilst he retained such feelings he would find the strength to carry on through the adversity. In an effort to avoid allowing whichever pernicious little shit had emailed him spoil his mood, he bypassed his laptop and, instead, poured himself a generous nightcap with the final dregs of last night's whisky bottle, which he enjoyed on his balcony before settling into bed with a serenity he hadn't experienced in years.

Chapter Twenty-four

The airport had an eerie feeling with so few flights allowed out between 11pm and 6am due to noise regulations. But Johnson had wasted no time in getting there and settled down in one of the uncomfortable seats close to the check-in desk, waiting for it to reopen in advance of the first flights to Alicante in the morning.

As soon as Brandt's wife had confirmed that, in the time she'd known him, he hadn't been able to speak a word of a foreign language, she began her search. Knowing that he would be looking for a longer-term home she put typical British holiday destinations to one side and focused on the key European areas for ex-pats. Gibraltar was her favoured location because, as an actual British territory, it was where she would have selected if she was looking for a home away from home. However, her attention switched to Benidorm, another of her targets, when she found out about the murder of an English woman who moved there a few years ago. It wasn't enough to act on because she was much older than his typical victim, and the method of killing was different to before, but this was the first murder in any of the places she had selected in the time since he had escaped to the continent that could possibly be attributed to him. Without him responding to her taunt about knowing it was he who had sent the email to the Belgian police, it had taken all her patience to remain in her impersonal flat, checking the various news feeds from the regions.

Then, finally, another one came up in Benidorm. Same method of killing, same sort of victim; far too much of a coincidence in Johnson's eyes. She hastily packed a bag and made her way down to retrieve her car. Eschewing the nearby East Midlands Airport, she favoured the long drive to Gatwick, not only because of the number of the flights to Alicante but the fact that they started as soon as the night time layoff ended. Although she was grateful for finding a spare seat on the first flight to depart for Spain, the exorbitant fee the woman from the so-called low-cost airline sheepishly quoted her almost caused her to balk. As she waited at the boarding gate, trying to drown out the noise from her fellow passengers, she swore to herself that this had better be worth it. She did manage to cheer herself up with an email she sent just before switching her phone onto airplane mode, as they taxied towards the runway.

With the flight only taking a couple of hours, it was still early as Johnson switched back on her data as she landed in Alicante. Although concerned that his lack of a response to her first message meant he wasn't checking the account he had set up specifically for informing the Belgian police, by the same token, she didn't want him answering her new one without her being in the position to reply immediately and engage him in a conversation.

As she waited throughout the long taxi journey into Benidorm, she reflected on what she would do if he continued to fail to make contact. It was now mid-morning and she had just checked into her hotel in the centre of the New Town, a modest but pleasant enough three-star affair, when the mail symbol on her phone indicated that she had received a message.

He had replied.

– Who are you?

It may have been in the subject bar like both the emails she had sent him, but he had favoured avoiding the aggressive tone implied by her sole use of capitals. She would reciprocate in kind, having finally engaged him with her claim that she now knew where he was.

– I want to help you.

– How?

The response was almost immediate, which was a sign to Johnson that she had him rattled.

– I believe you.

– How can you help me?

Johnson paused, her fingers hovering over the keypad. This was a curious reply. She wasn't surprised that he was being cautious with his responses because, for all he knew, she was bluffing. In actual fact she didn't yet know whether she had made the wrong assumption following reading the news stories. But she was in no doubt that this was Brandt she was speaking to and the realisation of this caused a shiver to run down her spine. Not only had he immediately dropped the subterfuge of typing in French, but he hadn't even asked what she supposedly believed him about.

– I can prove you weren't responsible.

– WHO ARE YOU???

Johnson took in a deep breath as she typed her reply. Whilst her actions to this point had been questionable, this was definitely crossing the line. However, as she had sat in her flat waiting for the news she required, this was the only way she could think of. She hadn't heard from Claire since her return from Belgium but, rather than it ease the tremendous pressure and sense of responsibility she felt, it only added to it. The thought that even Claire had given up on her, only made her more determined to do whatever it took to bring McNeil's killer to justice.

> — *Gail Trevelly*

A long pause this time, and Johnson was starting to fear that she had scared him off altogether. Even if he was in Benidorm, all she had to go on so far was that he was unlikely to be staying in a hotel because she had been asked for her passport on check-in.

> — *You wrote about me.*

A simple, almost innocuous statement, but she could sense the accusation contained therein. Whether she could maintain an effective dialogue depended on his reaction to her next message.

> — *I was tricked by DCI Johnson into running that story. I believe she has also tricked you.*

She could feel herself tingling in anticipation of what mentioning her name to him would provoke.

> — *Go on…*

> — *I think Nottingham was a set up. She had no evidence on you and conspired with PC McNeil to create a scene of incriminating evidence.*

It pained Johnson to type this; to allow Brandt the satisfaction of believing he had duped yet more people. Burying her hurt inside her, she wondered whether this was enough. Should she say more about this supposedly pre-constructed and artificial crime scene? She could claim that McNeil had let it slip to his sister that they had been planning to trap Brandt with the idea that he would supposedly arrive on a whim and catch him in the act. But Brandt had been extremely cautious so far in this conversation and to say more would overplay her hand. If he needed clarification, he would ask for it, and she would just have to see whether he took the bait.

— Why would she do that?

— Fame. When she spoke to me before I asked her why catching you was so important to her. She said she wanted to become famous like Maggie Oliver.

Johnson had put a lot of thought into this on the flight. She knew that if she got this far with Brandt, he was bound to ask why Gail Trevelly thought Johnson would risk her life to get a conviction. She had initially dismissed the idea of comparing herself to the DC from Preston who exposed the Rochdale child sex grooming scandal. Johnson believed her motivation had been entirely honourable, even if it did gain her the sort of exposure that saw her on last year's Celebrity Big Brother. However, she kept coming back to the idea because she realised that she was viewing the world through her own perspective and not that of the man she was pursuing. She didn't know what had caused him to become a serial killer, but he had an obvious disrespect towards women and, given how he had reacted to the newspaper article suggesting he may be bisexual, suffered from a large ego. Therefore, for him to judge people by his own low standards, it was perfectly conceivable that he would view Maggie Oliver as some fame-hungry media whore, who put herself above the integrity of the force.

— What now?

— Let me get your side of the story. I can't promise it will provide the police with the evidence they need to expose the plot against you, but it may help to get the truth out there.

— How do I know this isn't just a set up?

— Meet me in person. For me to put myself in the hands of a suspected serial killer would show my faith in your innocence.

— Why take the risk?

— Because I believe in truth. Not all of us journalists are crooked, you know!

Johnson thought carefully as to whether this sounded sincere enough and a sufficient motivation. It needed a little more, and the best way she had found to hide a lie was to disguise it with something more plausible.

— Plus, seeing as we're being honest, this could give me a significant leg up in my career.

— Send me your phone number.

Why? For what purpose? Is this a test? Any of these responses could appear defensive enough to make him suspicious. With a sigh she typed in her number. Whilst he may have the IT skills to hide IP addresses, she was sure he couldn't hack the phone companies to trace her number.

Her phone beeped from an incoming text message.

— Where do you propose we meet?

Jesus Christ, he might not be able to trace her number, but she could as long as she passed this on to the police. She didn't want to though, and reassured herself that even if he believed that it was Gail Trevelly that was contacting him then she could do the same. It wasn't worth blowing the whole thing in the unlikely belief that he would make what would appear such a monumental cock up by accident. Perhaps this was the real test. He would wait and see if the location of the mobile mast that was used to transmit the message was stormed by the police in the next hour or so, to see if the emails were genuine.

— Up to you.

— I thought you said you knew where I am…

Still cautious, which Johnson took as a good sign that he wasn't now just playing with her. But where could she suggest? She needed to buy herself time to think.

— Fine, play it your way.

It didn't really matter to her, she wasn't actually going to meet him. That would be stupid; even if he didn't manage to kill her on sight, she would then be up for a murder charge herself. Instead she would wait for him to arrive and then would follow him back to his place. There she would kill him, and the stuff she had written to him about her house in Nottingham hadn't just come to her mind in order to convince him that Gail Trevelly was on the level. She would make it look like he had lured her there and she had killed him in a desperate act of self-defence. Even if the police did suspect something, there would be no incentive for them to pursue it given the massive media exposure it would provoke. It wasn't as though they weren't already in the shit for having two senior officers responsible for a serial killing spree. She didn't care though; she would do whatever it took to make Brandt pay for what he had done. Even if it meant that her career would be over, it would be a small price to pay for the satisfaction of watching the life fade from his eyes in the same way she had been forced to watch McNeil's. She allowed herself a chuckle to think she may even appear on the next Celebrity Big Brother.

— So where then?

Keen not to test his patience any further, Johnson quickly accessed Google on her mobile browser and found a generic seafront bar.

— Well, I would say a landmark like The Cross overlooking Benidorm but you may think it's too

isolated. Let's just go for Sol Beach Bar. I hear the drink prices are very reasonable.

Johnson erased the last part; it was too flippant for someone who, despite what she was claiming, must be in some fear for her life.

— *What time?*

Here was the kicker. For her plan to work he would have to believe she still had to fly out from England. She needed to give the impression without making it look like that was exactly what she was doing.

She gazed at her watch and made some mental calculations.

— *I'll be there by 9pm.*

— *Don't be late.*

Johnson put her phone on the bed and sat back for a moment with adrenaline still coursing through her system. She had thought of little else over the past couple of weeks and now it was finally going to happen. She got up, needing a cigarette to calm her nerves, but more than that, she needed to get a move on.

Whilst sitting dozing at Gatwick, waiting for the check-in desks to open in advance of the first flights of the day, she had remembered the story of the three little pigs that she had been read as a child. She bought the book for her nephew when he had been small and, on one of the rare occasions when she visited her sister, read it to him for his bedtime story. But the version she purchased was not the same as the one she had been told as a child. In her nephew's book, when the wolf arrived at the first house, made of straw, and started huffing and puffing, he didn't blow it down and gobble up the little pig. In this story the pig ran away to the second house, made of sticks. Then, when the wolf huffed and puffed and blew that one down, they both escaped and went to the third pig's brick house.

There the wolf huffed and puffed and was unable to blow it down. And the three pigs lived happily ever after.

Her nephew had seemed satisfied enough, but Johnson had left his room disappointed. It wasn't so much that in the story she had been told as a child, the first and second pigs were gobbled up by the wolf as soon as he managed to blow their houses down, it was what the wolf did after he encountered the house made of bricks. Rather than just give up when he realised that no matter how much he huffed and puffed he wouldn't be able to blow it down, he then sought to lure the third pig out from the house by saying he knew a nice field of turnips. The little pig agreed to meet up at 6am but, instead, got up at 5am and had been to collect the turnips before the wolf arrived. The rest of the story where, after being tricked again, the wolf tried to gain entry to the house via the chimney, only to fall into a pot to be cooked for the pig's lunch, didn't interest Johnson as she waited at Gatwick. Brandt was the wolf and she was the cunning little pig who was going to trick him by providing a false time.

As Johnson left the hotel and stepped into the baking Spanish sunshine, she headed straight for the Sol Beach Bar, only stopping off at a kitchenware store to purchase a large knife, which she concealed in her bag. Regardless of how convincing she would have been, Brandt would be suspicious of a trap and she fully expected him to scope out the bar in advance. With him believing she was yet to fly out to Spain, he wouldn't be nearly as careful as she would tonight, and she would simply find a suitable vantage point for when he did rear his head, and then follow the wolf back to his lair.

Chapter Twenty-five

– Don't be late.

As soon as Brandt finished typing his final reply, he opened up a new web browser to find the location of the bar. The map provided a good overview of its surroundings, but he wanted to go and see it first-hand.

Having woken after nine hours' solid sleep, the calmness he had felt as he opened his eyes remained, even when he logged on to find that Trish's body had been discovered. He had known it was only a matter of time and, in a way, the anticipation of it happening was worse than the reality. He didn't even regret his decision not to check on his return last night. It wasn't as though he would have had many options for his escape at that hour and, this way, at least he was fully rested and able to think straight.

Clearly his six-hour estimate for the length of time had been far too pessimistic. It wasn't just the fact his door hadn't been kicked in whilst he serenely slept; he knew the timing of the discovery meant he could effectively start his countdown timer now. Even if they had gone to the effort of erecting those huge floodlights the forensics would have needed in order to scan the area at night, it would only be in the morning that they would be able to process the prints and DNA samples. So, Brandt figured it most likely they were still doing that now and there remained the time it would take them to contact the UK police, track Trish's movements that day, speak to the taxi driver and then begin their door-to-door search of the area where he had been picked up. It wasn't that he was complacent, he just didn't see the need to rush unnecessarily and, besides, he fully intended being out of Benidorm by lunchtime.

However, things had changed when he checked his email. It would seem his phantom messenger had worked as quickly as the authorities. He had thought she was just bluffing as to his location until he got her to suggest their meeting spot. He wasn't sure whether she was on the level, but it did give him an alternate plan. He had come to Benidorm to hide in plain sight, among the people who would know more about his exploits than anyone else. Now that he had made his false travel plans to Torremolinos, as long as he made his villa look like he had left in a hurry, he reasoned that the last place they would expect him to be was still in Benidorm. The other advantage of this plan was that it would give him the opportunity to find out whether what the woman was saying was true. He didn't know how she had made the connection between him and Benidorm so quickly after his crimes had been reported, but he was now absolutely certain that she wasn't acting in conjunction with the police. There was no way they would let her send a message that could have seen him running for the hills if they were so close to catching him.

With the only thing Brandt possessed of true value being his laptop, which he needed to leave behind as part of his subterfuge, he packed lightly before arranging the rest of his items around the villa in the necessary way. He had known the risk of accepting the owner's terms of three months' rent up front but, as he closed the door for the final time, the money he had wasted galled him. Sauntering down the road, leaving the trail from Trish's caravan behind him, he contemplated whether he should find his alternate accommodation before or after he had checked out this Sol Beach Bar. His bag was light, and he was enjoying the sunshine so much he settled on the latter. He was in no rush to get there, though, and headed straight for the seafront where he removed his shoes to enjoy the warm Mediterranean water as he paddled along the seafront in its direction. He even stopped occasionally to watch the various water skiers zipping back and forth sufficiently far out not to interfere with any of the swimmers.

His slow pace meant that there was no visible alteration to his demeanour as he neared his destination. Behind his dark glasses, none of the sunbathers would have detected the change in his eyes as they flicked from side to side searching for what he required.

And there it was, exactly where he expected to find it. Not outside the bar, or even anywhere directly in front of it, but a discreet distance further down the road, and with excellent lines of sight. The very place he would have chosen in fact. But he would have come better prepared, especially if he were choosing to go it alone like she clearly was; any notion of police back-up notable by its absence. There was nothing Brandt would have been able to do about the need to turn the lounger away from the sea but, he would have given the impression of not wanting to face the sun, by at least wearing sunglasses. Awkward as it may have been, he would also have picked one next to a family so, at a glance, he would appear as part of the group rather than stick out as one of the few loners on the beach. He tutted as he observed her bag, thinking that it wouldn't have taken much instead to lie out some clothes next to her as though her companion had nipped off for an ice cream or a quick drink.

Brandt continued to look at the bag and wondered as to its contents. Whilst she may have needed to keep it with her because she had yet to check-in anywhere, he considered what it might be concealing. A knife perhaps. Brandt pondered whether, if his own bag contained a knife, he would be able to creep quietly up the beach and run its sharp blade across her throat before she even realised someone was behind her. With her choking on her own blood, and unable to call out, he reckoned he could slip away before anyone noticed what had happened.

But he didn't have one. So, after a quick sigh of what might have been, Brandt turned and started retracing his steps along the shore front. 'Goodbye DCI Johnson,' he whispered under his breath.

Chapter Twenty-six

— What happened to you?

Johnson still clung onto the prospect that her plan hadn't failed. She had spent the whole day squinting through the searing hot sunshine at that fucking place. When he hadn't surfaced within a few hours she reasoned that she may have been so convincing in her messages that he hadn't felt the need to scope out the location in advance, but still she remained there; determined not to miss her opportunity. As the sunset caused people to leave the beach, she moved to another location; keeping her line of sight throughout. She had started to fear the worst when he didn't arrive by 9.30pm but had stayed there, alert, for a further hour; just in case.

She had chosen her words carefully once she returned to her hotel room, not daring to hope that the reason for his no-show was because he had been arrested, but he may have a good explanation and the last thing she wanted to do was blow her chance by becoming abusive. She had even resisted the temptation to text, believing that an email would seem less pushy.

— I'm sorry it was a wasted trip.

The ambiguity of his reply was deeply frustrating. Was it an apology for not having met up as agreed, or him implying that he would never meet her?

— *I wanted to help you.*

All she could do in the circumstances was try and remind him of what should motivate him.

— *And you did. You made me realise I need to be more careful in future.*

— *Because I made the connection?*

Johnson hoped he was just referring to how she knew it was him that had committed the murders in Benidorm.

— *You could say that.*

If she didn't already despise him, this smug response would have tipped her over the edge.

— *Where are you? Time to stop playing these stupid games.*

— *Oh, come now, you're smarter than that.*

She had barely read it when another email came through.

— *Although perhaps, Miss Johnson, not quite as smart as you think you are.*

Her blood ran cold. She felt sick to her stomach. Most of all, she felt afraid. She didn't know how he knew it was her, but she suddenly felt as vulnerable as when she had regained consciousness in her house to find herself tied naked to her bed. Certain that he must be waiting outside her room at that very moment, she leapt up and pushed the cheap wooden dresser in front of the door, doubting it would be strong enough to keep him out indefinitely, but she would be waiting, knife in hand. He may ultimately win but she wouldn't go down without a fight.

Chapter Twenty-seven

Johnson was woken up by the sun streaming through the gap in her curtains. She took a few moments to consider where she was; she didn't recognise the room, nor did she understand why she was sat up on the bed. The sight of the large kitchen knife in her lap brought everything immediately back to her. Staring at the door with the dresser still where she had moved it, wasn't enough for her to believe that Brandt hadn't somehow got in whilst she slept and was hiding somewhere; waiting to pounce. She had no doubt that it would be much worse this time, and not just in terms of how it would end. If the mocking tone in his last email was anything to go by, he would take even more pleasure in her suffering, and he would know there was no one to save her this time.

Despite checking every inch of her room and gingerly pulling back the shower curtain in the en-suite, she never felt truly settled. The rational part of her brain told her that, with people heading out for breakfast and staff starting to service the rooms, he would be mad to still be outside. Nevertheless, she waited until the cleaner, having first knocked, used his swipe card to enter before she ventured out. Hunger drove her down to the buffet restaurant where she struggled to find food that hadn't been deep fried. Feeling heavy with carbohydrates, she wanted nothing more than to leave and hail a taxi back to the airport but convinced herself it would be better to wait a little longer. Keen to avoid the confines of her room, she made her way to the poolside bar where she proceeded to chain smoke whilst consuming cup after cup of poor-quality coffee.

Feeling sick from the combined effects of the fatty food and too many stimulants, Johnson made her way back to her room. The paranoia of last night had faded and she felt no fear as she opened her door. Sitting on her bed contemplating whether to take a nap or just get on with packing for the airport, the sudden ringing of her mobile phone startled her. It was DSI Potter. He wanted to inform her that they had traced Brandt, but he had absconded before they could get to him. The lack of any specific details suggested a reluctance to offer information that Johnson didn't bother to challenge, given she knew what he was referring to. She detected a somewhat apologetic tone, but he never came close to admitting she had been right about him fleeing to Europe. With the message passed on, Potter was keen to draw the conversation to a close with only a superficial query as to how she was faring. Nevertheless, she welcomed his lack of warmth because, much as she resented the way he had treated her recently, she didn't feel comfortable lying to the man she had spent many years working with.

With the immediate threat having gone, Johnson experienced a mixture of emotions. Chief among them was humiliation; not at being outwitted by Brandt but that she had allowed him to gain such control over her by giving in to her fear. She had worked so hard to get to the stage where she could confront him but, because it would not have been on her terms, she had shrunk away from it. During the night, in the long hours until she could no longer resist sleep, she had thought of many messages to send him. Now she was pleased she hadn't, for they all would have added to that power; seeking as she would have done to gain reassurance that he wasn't waiting for her.

Partly through shame but mostly through a sense that she couldn't leave until at least she had tried to wrestle back some of the power that had been abandoned so easily last night, she began writing a new email. It was feeble, petulant even, but it did feel good for the first time not to write something subservient.

    — Running scared, are we?

As she waited for a response, she contemplated what he would read into it. Would he take it to mean she was aware that the place he had been staying at had been stormed by the police? Perhaps he might even think that, rather than cowering in her room all night, desperately clutching her knife and waiting for her barricade to be burst open, she had hunted the town for him. Even the mere chance that he might get that impression whilst he fled like the coward he was, made her start to feel better.

It was fleeting though, to be replaced by the knowledge that to allow something so petty and in the context of things infinitesimally small to give her a boost, only made her wonder what she had become. Perhaps Potter had been right in refusing to put her back on the case. That she was sat here trying to score points against a man, a cold-blooded serial killer in fact, proved that she was too emotionally involved to act rationally. But what else could she do? Just return to England and to the station as though she had been on a nice little holiday? Pretend she didn't mind what bullshit investigations she was placed on, whilst DI Fisher got the good stuff, because she was simply happy to still be alive and in the process of rebuilding her life? Enter the office each day and smile warmly at the people around her who were fucking up finding the person responsible for the death of the only man she had ever really cared for?

Johnson sat there for hours thinking about the futility of her situation and waited for an email that never came. Whatever connection she had managed to establish with Brandt yesterday had been severed. Not only had she blown her chance to get him, her intervention had served to tip him off that he was close to being caught and would only have caused him to be more careful in future. With all hope of exacting the righteous retribution she craved gone, but unable to accept that she could somehow seek to move on, at that point she had never felt more lost; more alone.

Chapter Twenty-eight

Brandt was annoyed. He was annoyed at many things but, most of all, he was annoyed at being annoyed. He knew he should be satisfied with the events of the previous day, but he had never been one for living in the moment. He was always looking towards the future. One of his mother's favourite sayings to him as a child was, if I gave you the moon, you'd want the stars as well, and it was only now that he accepted there may have been some truth in her words.

The fact was he was staying in a dingy bed-sit whose sole view was over-looking some industrial bins behind a restaurant. He had retired early, to keep a low profile whilst the police were searching the area following their unsuccessful storming of his, much larger and vastly superior, villa. But he had barely got any sleep, with the increasingly noisy revellers who had frequented the bars around him shouting and singing until the first rays of dawn were in the sky.

Even Johnson's email, which seemed to confirm the perception that he had long fled Benidorm, had failed to cheer him up. He had hoped his exchange with her last night, where he had revealed he knew her identity, would lead to her begging for her life. That would have gone some way to combating the deep regret he had felt walking away from her on the beach. He knew he couldn't put his inability to wait for her to leave down to bad luck, because she wouldn't have been there in the first place had it not been for his actions linking him to Benidorm. Johnson may have made the connection sooner than the police, but the two were inextricably linked. Yet that hadn't stopped him fantasising about following her back to whichever hotel she was staying at and finishing the job from Nottingham.

The email exchange that had followed that night, where he could sense her desperate refusal to accept her plan went wrong and almost feel the pain with which she typed her efforts to placate him, had provided a little comfort. But now she just seemed to be goading him. He wanted to respond and tell her he hadn't fled and was still in Benidorm but, even if she believed him, it could cause him problems in the long run. Although she had been acting alone, it only highlighted her desperation to catch him; one that could see her turn back to the police if she now thought it the best way. Therefore, to reveal he was still in Benidorm could place him in danger.

In many respects he wished he had run away. His ability to turn the bad situation of the caravan site around into that magical evening he had spent at the cabaret now seemed a distant memory. That should have been the thing he held on to when he thought of Benidorm, but it would be sullied by his current existence. It wasn't just his accommodation; even though the police believed him to be elsewhere, he knew he would have to be warier when he did finally go out. Worse than that, all hopes of him finding a companion here were gone. In a twist of irony considering the fear he had sought to spread in England, he knew that middle-aged women in the ex-pat community would be more cautious of strange men talking to them. Naturally things would eventually die down, as the complacency that blighted society set in once more, but whatever hopes he had held for being happy there had evaporated.

The alternative would be to simply leave. He would need to wait a couple of days for the dust to settle and the police to stop monitoring the various routes out. But to do so would be to add credence to Johnson's taunt. It disturbed him that he cared so much about what she thought. Surely his humiliation of her yesterday, added to the knowledge of what he did to her in her own home, should be enough to not feel threatened by her. But just as he didn't like the way her icy blue eyes had seemed to be boring into him when he had first seen her on television at the press conference, he resented how she was able to get so close to him. She had been the one who had seen through his email to the Belgian police and, more disturbingly, she must have known it was him who was responsible for Trish's death the moment the news was broken. It didn't worry him that the police came to the same conclusion because he knew how they worked. He had known that he had left DNA at the scene that they would trace back to him, and his understanding of their processes made him confident that, even if he continued to make mistakes, he would always manage to stay one step ahead of them. The trouble with Johnson was that he didn't know how she worked and that made her a danger to him. He had been lying in last night's message when he claimed she wasn't as clever as she thought she was. It may have been true in the context of her plan to lure him into the open under the pretence of a newspaper article that would somehow absolve him of his sins, but she possessed a rare and unique ability; he recognised that she had the same sixth sense that he did when investigating crimes. He had been able to get into the mind of the murderers he was hunting and used that, not only to better understand why they had done those terrible things, but to predict what they were going to do next. Johnson hadn't relied on science to establish the link between him and the killings here; she had done so on instinct. Moreover, she must have been actively looking for that link, which meant she had already suspected he may have been in Benidorm.

Which was why yesterday seemed like a hollow victory to Brandt. Johnson may not have got quite as close to him as she thought she had, but it had been close nonetheless. That she had been willing to put her career, perhaps her liberty, and even her life on the line to do so worried Brandt. He had never gone to anything like such lengths when he had been chasing someone. He understood that, clearly, he was somewhat responsible for this situation, because of what he had done to her, but the fact was she was the one who had made it personal. He would never have tracked her down had she not orchestrated that salacious newspaper article. If that wasn't bad enough, to then, not only have the temerity to pose as its author, but to use it as a way to lure him back in, demonstrated she would do anything, no matter how distasteful, to win.

Perhaps yesterday had wounded her even more than the events in Nottingham, but Brandt knew that this was when a beast was at its most dangerous. He dreaded to think what she would make of the details of Trish's murder. The police would make it public that they believed it to be sexually motivated but that would only spur her on to find out all the sordid details. Brandt wasn't ashamed of what had happened; given the woman's behaviour, it was perfectly understandable that she was unable to arouse him. If only he had taken advantage of how seeing her life slipping away from her had made him feel. Without having done anything to her post-mortem he could just imagine how Johnson would view it. The article from before may have just been a desperate shot in the dark to try and crack a case that was beyond her, but she would see the events in the caravan as legitimising her claims.

With dawning horror Brandt came to understand what her next move would be. Johnson would think she had lost him for good. He had stated as much last night when he said she had taught him to be more careful in future. She wouldn't just accept it was over and try and move on, as he had hoped she had done following their encounter at her house. She would be angry. She would refuse to accept her own culpability and, instead, seek to lash out. Knowing that she could no longer get to him by hunting him down, she would revert to the only way she had managed to hurt him in the past.

It wouldn't matter that he had proven to her that he wasn't impotent or a homosexual. He might not have fucked her in Nottingham but there was no doubting she saw his erection as he straddled her on the bed. She would lie to the press about his virility and use the crime scene at the caravan to somehow prove it. No smoke without fire, and it would stick this time. What made it inextricably worse was how Susan would react. Despite being livid before, thoughts of his ex-wife hadn't come into it, because at that point his identity had still been unknown. He hadn't really considered it since, but deep down he hoped that she had simply been unaware of what had been going on until his name had been mentioned. But there would be no avoiding it this time. It would stir up a media frenzy and she would face questions about their sex life every time she opened her front door.

This was the worst of it for Brandt, but not due to any sense of the huge discomfort it would cause Susan. Indeed, quite the opposite. She had caused him to start doubting his ability to perform and, not only would these reports make it a self-fulfilling prophecy, but she would also see it as legitimising her leaving him and abandoning their sacred vows of marriage.

This was all too much to bear. The suicidal thoughts that had been absent for so long came flashing back to him. He would leave now and head up to The Cross that Johnson had referred to yesterday. Up on the cliffs overlooking Benidorm he could fulfil his fantasy of plunging to his death and all this pain would go away.

But he knew that it would stop nothing. Johnson would have won. She would resent him for taking away her chance at retribution and be all the more determined to spread her deceitful filth. With every possible option, even death, seeming to lead to the same inevitable outcome, Brandt broke down and cried. He sobbed until his voice became hoarse and no more tears would come. Lying on his bed, his mind fractured with despair, eventually the sleep that evaded him last night pulled him down into a few hours of blissful unconsciousness.

With the starting up of the disco next door, he opened eyes still blurred from his earlier tears. Wiping away the snot which had not yet dried on his chin, he picked up his phone. He very much doubted that Johnson would choose to involve the police at this stage and, anyway, they would be bound to assume he sent it before making his final escape. Much more important was his need to reach out to her and for her to see it before it was too late.

> *— Don't you dare spread any more lies. You know what I am capable of.*

Chapter Twenty-nine

'Jesus Christ,' Johnson whispered to herself. In the moment of reading that text, her dreadful experience in Benidorm and the desolate trip home, which had felt like retreating in defeat, instantly evaporated. With Brandt having failed to reply to her last, desperate email, she was sure her arrival back on British soil marked the end of her chances of encountering him again. Yet these two sentences were a potential game changer.

She knew what they were designed to do, but the barely veiled threat only worked to convince her that all was not lost. She had no idea what had provoked him into such an outburst, but was determined to exploit any weakness. Gone was the calm smugness that had signalled his toying with her; he was genuinely scared of something. But what? Don't you dare spread any more lies. That could only be a reference to the article that she had prompted Gail Trevelly to write. Though surely, if he had sought to hide this concern whilst he was still pretending to believe it was her who was emailing him, it would have come out during the exchange following the no-show. What had changed in those hours since, whilst she had been feeling like a virtual prisoner in her hotel room?

Minutes passed without her being able to come up with a single plausible explanation. She then tried to distract herself by switching on the television in the hope that, in the same way as when she was unable to come up with a specific word, not thinking about it would reveal the answer. But it was all to no avail. The sudden hope that she had greeted his message with was rapidly fading, and she started to believe that, once again, her inability to successfully fathom what Brandt was up to signalled she could never expect to catch him.

Nevertheless, she would not let go of this unexpected lifeline and focused on the notion of lies. It still made sense to her that if he was referring to anything that had been shared between them yesterday, then it would have come out in their conversation. Therefore, it had to be something different. It crossed her mind that it could be regarding her taunt about him running away but she couldn't see how his evading the police once more would be such a source of embarrassment. Unquestionably, he would view it as the same kind of victory as tricking her into thinking he had fallen for her ruse. So, what could he have done that he was frightened about being made public?

He must have done something he was ashamed of. But then it would be completely stupid to shoot himself in the foot by revealing to his nemesis the very chink in his armour that he was so desperate to conceal. This was, perhaps, unless he believed she already knew or, at the very least, soon would. She double checked the news feeds from the area to make sure nothing had broken in the time since she left the hotel. Whilst not discounting the possibility altogether, Johnson felt it unlikely he was referring to a crime that had yet to be discovered. It made sense that he would wait, like with St. Albans, in the hope that it wasn't linked to him.

Which just left one possibility; it was something he had done that was already known about. She looked back to the first murder, the one that had alerted her to the prospect he might be in Benidorm. The details were thin, but it seemed that the attack was swift and, albeit by a different method, similar to those characterising his random attacks in England. Finding nothing of any use, she switched to the one at the caravan park. She was frustrated to find that the original article, the one which had prompted her to head for the airport, had been replaced now that Brandt had been identified as the culprit. It offered plenty of speculation as to his specific motivation, but she knew she couldn't trust it, as the author's thoughts would have been heavily influenced by his knowledge of Brandt's previous crimes.

She desperately tried to think back to what she had read that night. Written for its English-speaking audience, it had contained the sort of stock phrases she had used so many times in her career. It wasn't just their familiarity that had failed to cause her to pay much attention, but also her keenness at the time to act on it. She hunted around the internet, knowing there were plenty of piss poor so-called news sites that effectively just copied and pasted what they read elsewhere. She would need to locate one sufficiently useless that they hadn't yet updated theirs with the latest version. It would seem that these were more of a phenomenon in Britain, but it didn't take her too long to find what she was looking for.

It was disappointingly bland, and Johnson was about to give this line of enquiry up as being a blind alley, when she found her eyes drawn back to a particular phrase. 'It appears not to be motivated by financial gain.' The announcement had come so soon after the body's discovery that it seemed a little early to be ruling things out, even if the victim's purse had been found and the place hadn't been turned over. It may have been the case that her attacker had been looking for something of specific value, perhaps a piece of jewellery he had identified that had led to her becoming a target. Therefore, unless the Benidorm police were incompetent, which was always possible, that statement could only have come because they believed there had been a different motivation, one that they were not yet comfortable with revealing.

In Johnson's mind that could only be one thing. And that thing would explain, if not the timing, the reason behind Brandt's text message outburst; especially as it directly related to what had caused him so much angst previously.

She picked up her phone. She would require the specific details if she was going to exploit this situation to the full. The only people who would know were the people currently investigating it but contacting DSI Potter was out of the question. So too was DI Fisher because he would not want to do anything to endanger his current standing.

'Who is it?' The irritated tone was of someone being disturbed from their sleep. It was a risk Johnson had been willing to take because she knew she didn't have the patience to wait until morning.

'Hardy, it's me.'

'Ma'am?'

She wasn't surprised by the confusion in his voice. DC Hardy was one of the more junior members of CID and she had never had cause for contacting him outside of working hours. But he had been the first person to spring to mind. He had always been loyal and, despite only ever having played with a straight bat, she sensed that he did what he thought was right rather than what would make him popular with his superiors. There were other detectives with whom she had worked for much longer, and had built up more of a rapport, but with the winds of favour against her, she couldn't be sure any of them would be willing to do anything that would incur Fisher's displeasure.

That didn't mean Hardy would prove a push-over though. 'I need some information and, before you say anything, none of it can get you into any trouble.'

'What is it?' He sounded far from convinced.

'I need you to tell me everything you know about the crime scene at the caravan park in Benidorm.'

'Look, ma'am, I really think you should be talking to someone else about this.'

'I'm talking to you.' Perhaps a little pressure would help. Despite what had happened, she remained his superior and she knew he was still trying to prove himself within the team.

An awkward silence followed, one Johnson was determined she was not going to break first.

'I'm really not sure I should be talking to you at all.'

She smiled. Hardy was still protesting but, having won that little battle of who would speak, she knew he would crack eventually. A soft approach and reassurance that he wouldn't be doing anything improper would take time and she had wasted enough of it already.

'Look Hardy, this whole Brandt thing has turned into a complete fuck up. Remember I said all along he was abroad, whilst you lot were pissing about looking for him in England. And that was before you bought into the ridiculous notion that he was somehow an unfortunate pawn in Franklin's game. He's going to keep killing and someone's going to have to take the fall for all the incompetence. Do you think that's going to be Fisher? Or is it far more likely they'll use the person newest to the team and with the least experience as their scapegoat?' She stopped to allow everything to sink in and took his fast and heavy breathing as an indication that it had. 'If you give me what I need, which is nothing more than I couldn't find out myself if I came into my office tomorrow, you have my promise that I will fight to ensure that doesn't happen.'

'What is it you want to know?'

'That's the spirit, Hardy,' she replied cheerfully, not feeling in the slightest bit guilty for having to go so heavy on him.

'Well, well, well,' she said to herself smugly, ending the call. It would seem that Brandt had been a very naughty boy after all. She could see how it wasn't so much fear of the information getting out that had driven him to threaten her, but how it could be twisted to apparently confirm the very thing that had caused him so much upset before. There was no doubt the police would not choose to release the full details of what had gone on in the caravan; it wasn't in the public interest. As a matter of fact, Brandt might welcome their heavily abridged description of it being sexually motivated. Much as he had sought to do to her, he would feel that this would disprove the notion that he was having issues with his sexuality and that his failure to function properly when in the company of women was driving his desire to kill.

But even if the public didn't appreciate the distinction between a sexually motivated attack and a sexual assault, Johnson did. From what Hardy had told her, the physical contact prior to the strangulation had been consensual. Brandt had performed oral sex on the woman, with no signs of struggle. The absence of any pre-ejaculate in her mouth suggested that if she had reciprocated he hadn't been aroused, backed up by there being no evidence of penetration. Moreover, it wasn't just his DNA that was found at the crime scene; his fingerprints were present too. He must have used gloves with his first attack in Benidorm, so it made no sense for him to be so reckless with this second one unless the killing itself wasn't premeditated.

Johnson laughed at herself for getting so carried away. She was still in detective mode – seeking to uncover the truth. She had to remind herself that it didn't really matter whether any of it was consensual or not, what did matter was how it could be made to look. She didn't have to concern herself with proving anything beyond reasonable doubt, all she had to do is make sure she had something juicy enough for her favourite columnist.

'Gail Trevelly,' came the reply after a few rings. Johnson smiled at the difference between her professionalism and Hardy's. It would seem that news never slept.

'Hi, Gail, it's Stella Johnson.' Her somewhat informal greeting was more than just trying to reignite their prior relationship. Although she didn't expect Gail to take it as such, she didn't want to use her title and sound like she was calling on official business, despite the ungodly hour.

'DCI Johnson, what can I do for you?'

It was fine for her to use it.

'Sorry to call you at this time of night but I thought you might appreciate a story that might be in time for one of the later runs.'

'Go on.'

'I have the perfect follow-up story for the one you ran on Brandt before.'

'Yes?'

Johnson wasn't rattled by Trevelly's apparent lack of enthusiasm. She told her everything she knew about the crime scene, off the record of course, and explained, without bothering to qualify any of her statements in case it made them sound like conjecture, how it proved that Brandt was indeed impotent. She even suggested a headline she believed to be suitable. Having finished her monologue, she sat back and sparked up a cigarette despite the no smoking clause in her tenancy agreement.

'So, Gail, what do you think?' She waited for the gratitude of a career-defining story to gush forth.

'Look, I appreciate you telling me this, but it all sounds a bit samey.'

'You what?'

'Well, it's not really anything I didn't write before.'

'Bullshit, Gail. What you wrote before was an implication that he might be a limp-dick. This proves it. Plus, what with all the furore surrounding the murders being committed by an ex-copper, it's bound to sell.'

'DCI Johnson, don't get me wrong. I'm grateful for what you did for me before. The exposure it got me was… well… useful. But the truth is I'm not really into that kind of journalism…'

'Fuck me, you're not starting to get all holier than thou on me, are you?!'

'…and so, I've tried to use my increased profile as a springboard onto better things,' she continued, as though she had not been interrupted. 'Like I said, I'm not ungrateful, and I may know some colleagues who might be interested in your story.'

'My story?'

'Well, of course, they would be interested in your theories about Brandt's motivation, if they were to add to that with you providing… details of your own experience then I'm sure you could come to some form of arrangement.'

Johnson couldn't believe what she was hearing. It was a far cry from when Gail had virtually begged her to expand on what she had said in the press conference. Now, the jumped-up bitch was not only going to pass on this sure-fire winning story, she was also suggesting she would need to prostitute herself to other journalists with the sordid details of her own attack.

The long pause that followed wasn't a ploy by Johnson to get her to speak again. She was fighting with herself not to just tell her to fuck off and, figuratively, slam down the phone. *Whatever it takes.* Those three words came back to haunt her, but Johnson found some encouragement from them. Given everything she had been through, swallowing her pride and pandering to this woman's narcissistic tendencies would hardly be too big a cross to bear.

However, in the face of such forbearance what could she offer her to make her reconsider?

'What if I could get his ex-wife to give you an exclusive?'

'Ah come now, Detective Chief Inspector, you know that's not possible.' The patronising laugh that followed, more than the words themselves, caused Johnson to seethe with anger. Nevertheless, she knew the basis for Trevelly's flippancy. Mrs Brandt had turned down every request for an interview, including a reported five figure sum from one of the television breakfast shows.

'It is,' she replied coolly. 'And all I need from you right now is your assurance that when I arrange it, you will make yourself available.'

'You have it.' No more sanctimony, just a simple statement delivered with sincerity.

Johnson ended the call at that point. She was still outraged but chief among her emotions was the anxiety at how she was going to deliver on her promise. Just getting his ex-wife to confirm on the phone that Brandt didn't speak any foreign languages had been tricky enough. Exhausted and in desperate need of sleep as Johnson was, she would need to think very carefully how she was going to approach this in the morning.

Chapter Thirty

Johnson hadn't dared phoning ahead and made the substantial drive down to Brandt's ex-wife in the knowledge she may find that she had gone out. A small cowardly part of her hoped it would be the case, but she knew that without the newspaper article she was otherwise out of ideas.

Pulling up at the address she'd had the foresight of noting down when she had snuck into the police station the night she looked for her phone number, Johnson was pleasantly surprised to see a lack of press camped outside. For whilst exposure was the whole point of her visit, she felt she could well do without her face being splashed all over the papers. She wanted Brandt to know who was behind this but wished for the connection to be a little subtler. However, the downside of there being no media attention there was it confirmed Gail Trevelly's claim that his ex-wife would be a tough nut to crack. If they even had the slightest inclination that she might relent and give them a story, they would be outside hounding her every move.

Johnson approached the front door of the modest but well-presented property with the decision that she would gain entry by implying she was there on police business.

She would make it sufficiently vague so that it was deniable should a complaint be made, but strong enough that Brandt's ex-wife would feel compelled to invite her inside.

Having rung the doorbell, she cleared her throat and waited. Through the frosted glass she eventually saw a shadow of someone silhouetted against the light from the back windows and avoided pressing the buzzer again for fear of appearing antagonistic. But her patience soon ran out and she started knocking instead. With that prompting another glimpse of movement, but it failing to result in someone approaching the door, Johnson was left with little choice unless she was prepared to walk away.

'Mrs Brandt!' she called. Shit, I should have checked whether she had changed her name following the divorce. 'It's DCI Johnson. Please can you open the door, so I can speak with you?'

'Go away!' The shout that came from within was more pleading than it was commanding.

'Please, Mrs Brandt. I really need to talk to you.'

There was a slow movement towards her and then a long pause at the door as though she was having second thoughts whether to open it. 'What do you want?'

'I think it's better if we discuss this inside.' Although Mrs Brandt was closer, Johnson had deliberately raised her voice in the hope that concerns for her privacy may prompt her into ushering her in.

As the door swung open, she could see the recognition on her face even before she spoke. 'What are you doing here?'

Johnson eased her foot into the door before responding. She had got this far and wasn't going to let this woman change her mind and ruin the plan. 'Mrs Brandt, could I possibly come inside?'

'Call me Susan,' she said, but her cold delivery suggested that requesting the use of her first name was not in order to appear friendly.

'I'm Stella,' Johnson replied holding out her hand and watching Susan reluctantly take it. This was a good sign: she might be unwelcome, but the woman's manners suggested she may well hear her out.

Guiding her through into the sitting room, Susan indicated that she would like Johnson to sit in the armchair while she took her position on a fairly new black leather sofa. 'I would offer you a drink, but I doubt you'll be staying long.'

'I don't wish to take up too much of your time,' she replied, in an effort to preserve whatever cordiality had been established.

'I know what he did,' Susan said flatly. 'To you, I mean.'

The bluntness of her words came as a shock and Johnson could feel her cheeks start to flush. She couldn't think of an appropriate response and waited for her to continue.

'Why are you here?'

In other circumstances Johnson would have admired how that bold opening statement had created a situation where she could no longer avoid the question that had already been asked a couple of times. However, Susan's vacant expression suggested that she wasn't playing a game, rather just speaking her mind.

'Susan, I need your help.'

'I'm sorry,' she said. 'I've told the police all I know. I guess they must believe I'm holding something back if they sent you round.'

'Why is that?' She couldn't help but ask the question.

'I guess the idea is that if I came face to face with one of his... his victims, it might shock me or something.'

This wasn't going how she had expected, and Susan was acting very differently to how she'd behaved when she had phoned her to establish whether Brandt spoke any foreign languages. She had been awkward, almost to the point of unhelpfulness, but here she just seemed resigned;

empty. Johnson knew she could exploit her current mood to extract information, but she would need there to be more emotion if she were to get her to agree to talking to Gail Trevelly.

'Do you smoke, Susan?' She already knew the answer; the way she was fiddling with her fingers was a giveaway that they wanted to do something else. The room didn't smell of tobacco but her going into the back garden to light up would explain the movement she saw through the door earlier.

'I do. So what?' Defensiveness mixed with a hint of confusion. Not where Johnson needed her to be yet, but anything was better than her cold delivery so far.

'I was wondering whether I could offer you a cigarette. I know I could do with one.'

After a few moments she could see Susan considering her proposition. Johnson knew that she could often appear aloof and, whilst that sometimes proved advantageous, in this situation she believed it helpful to seem more normal. It was easy to tell by her earlier answer that Susan's bravado was disguising her discomfort with her habit, and she wondered whether Brandt had disapproved of her smoking. It certainly seemed to be the norm these days and Johnson hoped that admitting her own addiction would help to form a bond.

'We'll need to go into the garden,' Susan replied, her tone implied mere tolerance of the suggestion, something subsequently undermined by the long, satisfied drag she took when they were both sat on the cheap plastic furniture either side of the overflowing ashtray perched on the low wall dividing the patio from the lawn.

Johnson waited whilst they both concentrated on the pleasurable act of smoking.

'Do you know why he attacked me?' she asked eventually, noting how her words caused Susan to sit up straight.

'No! Like I told them, I haven't even seen Jeff for three years now.'

Jeff. Hearing his first name used was peculiar. It made him sound almost human. Perhaps he had been when married. 'Why did you leave him?'

'I told them that too.'

'I mean, I want to know why you really left him.' Johnson hadn't seen any of the interviews, much less knew what had been said, but from her experience, even under extreme circumstances, people were reluctant to talk about their personal feelings. What came out was usually a sanitised, almost perfunctory statement of things that had happened rather than why they had occurred.

'He wasn't the man I married anymore.'

Johnson took another drag to imply she found the answer acceptable. It wasn't anywhere near good enough, but she had to take this softly to avoid causing Susan to shut down. 'What was your reaction when you found out what he had done?'

'I was shocked of course! Why, what do you think I am?'

Johnson ignored the challenge. 'Were you surprised?'

'Come again?'

'Did you think that there must have been some sort of a mistake. That somehow the police had suspected the wrong person?' Johnson waited patiently whilst Susan continued to smoke; her hand now shaking to the extent that she almost missed her lips.

'No,' she replied quietly.

'Why did you leave him, Susan?' she repeated with a firmness in her voice this time.

'I was scared.'

'Of him?'

'Yes.'

'Did he ever hurt you?' Johnson believed she knew the answer but needed to hear what would come next.

'No. But I knew he had become dangerous.'

Johnson concentrated on the remains of her cigarette, knowing that the groundwork had been sufficiently laid and she wouldn't need to ask anything more for Susan to explain what she meant.

'He lost himself; what was inside, you know? I used to think he was feeling guilty about us not being able to have children. It wasn't his fault, but I know he believed it was. Don't get me wrong, I wanted children too, but it stopped being about that... In the end I wanted a baby just to bring him back.' She sighed. 'I guess I didn't help. The more I tried to get pregnant the more pressure it piled on him.'

In that moment Johnson knew, despite everything Brandt had done, his ex-wife still loved him. She expected to feel revulsion at yet another abused woman somehow thinking it was her own fault, but all she felt was pity. 'Used to think?' she asked, referring back to something Susan had said that she had almost failed to spot.

'Well, in the beginning, he used to bury himself in his work. He'd come home late and find any excuse to get back to the office. And then he just stopped. He started working normal hours, even when there was a big case on. Not that he talked to me anymore about the investigations; I used to have to watch the local news to get any sort of clue what he was up to. It was as though he didn't care anymore. He'd loved his job. That dedication, that need to do good with his life, was a big reason why I fell for him. He then started talking about retirement when his earliest opportunity was still a few years off. The way he spoke about it was like a prisoner looking forward to his release date.' She paused to light a fresh cigarette. 'He was hollow. Empty. I tried to fill him back up with love again, but he wouldn't have it, he would barely go near me. Unless he was drunk, and it was only then I saw that there were two possible outcomes. Either the emptiness inside would end up killing him or he would look to fill it up with something else. Something... bad.'

Johnson felt pain at this woman's anguish. She wanted to hug her and say it was okay. She needed to tell her, before she said it herself, that she wasn't responsible for what he went on to do; that not being surprised by it didn't mean she could have predicted it, much less prevented it. But what she was here to do was more important than either of their feelings, and if she were going to achieve it, she needed Susan to continue down this dark road. *Whatever it takes.*

'Something bad?'

'I didn't expect it to be anything like that!' Susan shouted.

But? Johnson thought to herself.

'But I knew it would be bad. I said it was like he didn't care anymore. That was wrong; it was worse. It was as though he hadn't just given up on us, he had given up on everything. It was like the world was too broken for it to be fixed and his belief in that was what had made him empty inside.'

'Do you think he is punishing people for this now?'

She could see Susan was deep in thought, with minute changes to her facial expression as she fully considered the question. 'I've thought about little else than why he's doing it,' she said eventually. 'But the truth is I just don't know. Ten years ago, I would have said he didn't have a bad bone in his body, and I can't help but wonder whether he, in some fucked up way, thinks he is doing the right thing.'

Time to bring this back rather than allow her more opportunity to somehow find a justification for his actions. The look of shame that followed Johnson's next question confirmed that was exactly what Susan had been doing: 'Do you know why he attacked me?' She didn't wait for an answer. 'Because I got to him. I couldn't find him, so I provoked him.' Now was not the time to share that it had gone so differently to how she had anticipated.

'With that newspaper article?'

'Exactly. Without that, I think he would have kept on killing people here. I take it you are aware of what he's done in Spain?' Johnson allowed Susan's nod to be enough. 'He will keep on doing it if we don't stop him.'

'We?'

'Yes,' Johnson replied flatly. 'I need you to talk to a reporter.'

What followed was twenty minutes of bitter confrontation; a confrontation Johnson would have lost had it occurred when she first entered the house. Through the tears they both shed, at times from frustration and at others through misery, she knew that Susan couldn't deny their earlier conversation. Even if she didn't feel her irrational guilt for what Brandt had done, she, like Johnson, couldn't live with herself if she didn't take an opportunity to try and save some lives. And yet it had taken a huge amount of persuasion, even to the point that Johnson had to describe not only what he had done to that woman in Benidorm, but what he had also done to her.

She had delivered the knock-out blow by going through exactly what had happened in her house in Nottingham in much more detail than she had told the police. She left nothing out and she could see her wince as she spoke about him sat on top of her, his penis poking through his unzipped flies, and biting her nipple. It was obvious Susan wanted to tell her, to beg her, to stop but she was too transfixed by discovering the full extent of the monster her beloved husband had become.

Three hours later Johnson left the house, exhausted. Some of her own humanity had been lost through that exchange, but it had not only served to get Susan to agree to Gail Trevelly coming around for an interview, she also allowed herself to be briefed on what to say. Johnson drove back to her flat, barely aware of the traffic around her, reminding herself that it didn't matter how much of what was said was true, all that mattered was the effect it had on Brandt. She had no idea where he now was or what he was up to; but in a matter of hours his world would come crashing down.

Chapter Thirty-one

Brandt became aware something was wrong when he went to the local supermarket. He was there when it opened – whilst most of Benidorm remained asleep – so as to encounter as few people as possible. After 24 hours, he could see no signs of an increased police presence, but he still wanted to keep as low a profile as possible until he finally decided what he was going to do. And yet he had welcomed the fact his limited supplies necessitated a trip out, for the flat now seemed much worse than the dingy run-down shit hole he first believed it to be. Now it resembled little more than a prison cell and even just a few minutes in the early morning air felt a blessed relief.

He wouldn't have taken much notice of the hushed conversation he could barely overhear, were it not for the fact that the two people conducting it were huddled over the newspaper stand. Despite it only being two days since having sent Johnson the email, he knew it was just paranoia that made him think there was a chance that what these people were reading had anything to do with him. Unable to work out any more of what they were saying without getting close enough to disturb them, he left the supermarket and headed for a different shop in order to look at the newspapers himself.

What greeted him caused vomit to rise in his throat. It took enormous will for him to swallow it back down again and stagger to the counter to purchase the offending item. There on the front page was a photograph of Susan. Next to her was the headline: Ex-wife of notorious serial murderer exclusively reveals what drove him to kill.

He didn't want to read what was inside but knew he had no choice. Retaining just enough rationality to accept that he could not do so whilst out in public, he headed straight back to his apartment; tears streaming down his face.

'How... how could you?' he croaked in a small voice, having read the article for the third time. He simply couldn't believe it; what was being reported was far worse than he could ever have imagined. When Brandt started his new career, he had known there was a chance something like this would happen. His hope had been that he would have got sufficiently far with his plan that Susan would have understood that he'd achieved more to help society in the last few months than he had in his whole lifetime in the force. Johnson may have cut short that possibility, but he had taken Susan's steadfast refusal to do any interviews as a sign that she at least didn't condemn what he had done. For her to, not only agree to an in-depth interview, but then tell blatant lies was far worse than any of the crimes he had committed. He had only acted for the good of the people whereas she had deliberately set out to hurt him.

Well, perhaps she hadn't set out to. This had Johnson's stink all over it and not because she had been responsible for that other, as it turned out, far milder article. Even if it wasn't for the fact that Gail Trevelly was the author, with her smarmy professionally taken portrait sat proudly in the top corner, no one else could have put his wife up to it. His blood boiled at the thought of her at Susan's house;

the same fucking house he had to pay for as part of the divorce settlement, feeding her those lies. But Susan wasn't blameless in all of this. No matter what Johnson had said to her, no matter how elaborate her own lies were, she should have refused. She had betrayed him, and her betrayal could not go unanswered.

A certain tranquillity came over Brandt that reminded him of reports he had read about how some terminally ill patients felt when they received bad news. To have your very worst fears confirmed, can have the effect of silencing all those anxious voices. Concern had become cold, hard reality. Rather than worrying about what might happen, now that it had, he could focus on how to deal with it.

As he moved around his small bed-sit, collecting up his few possessions, he wondered whether it was always meant to come to this. Despite his best efforts, he was destined to confront the person responsible. Perhaps that had been why he had failed to settle in Benidorm; why fate had sent him that slut to show him he would never be able to move on and be happy. That's why he hadn't left and gone somewhere else: there was nowhere else to go except back to England.

For that was where Brandt was heading now as he exited the place that had become his prison cell over the last couple of days. Free from worrying about what might happen and what he should do, he had a purpose once again. There would be no planning of his route home or his method of transport. If this was truly what he was meant to do, then that same fate which had conspired to snatch his chance at happiness away from him, should also ensure he made it back safely. For whatever his future held, whether that be death or glory, it certainly didn't mean being arrested by the Spanish or French police.

Brandt walked down the street with his head held high. No one was going to spot him; no one was going to see the man concealed behind the dark glasses, straggly beard and deep tan. He had been wrong; it wasn't about the people. This was simply about himself, Susan and DCI Johnson. Everyone else was just there to provide context for the true stars of this feature and, aside from those who had given up their lives, they would be the uncredited extras that were barely noticed, much less remembered afterwards.

An hour later, sat in the cab of a lorry whose driver's grasp of English was as good as Brandt's was of Spanish, and enjoying the silence that resulted, he switched on his phone. He didn't care that, if tracked, it would show he had been moving in a northerly direction. He wanted Johnson to know he was coming for her. He wanted her to feel that fear and apprehension that had plagued him so many times. But she wouldn't be granted the calmness he felt now. When she realised that her anxieties had come true, all she would then feel is nothing as she entered the oblivion that surely followed life. For Brandt was certain there was no God; no almighty creator who had put man on this Earth and was watching over him. No sense of religion could survive if people could see the horrors and callous acts of brutality he'd witnessed.

Six words to start the process that would see DCI Johnson become a mere footnote in the history Brandt was creating. No need for profanity in an attempt to emphasise his intentions.

— *I warned you what would happen.*

Chapter Thirty-two

Johnson had woken early to collect a copy of the paper from the local newsagents. She was anxious to see exactly what had been written because Gail Trevelly had still been playing the hard-arse and had refused to send her a draft. Johnson had not bothered to push the matter because she had sat in during the whole interview. She hadn't even needed to ask; Susan had insisted that she be there. The notion that she was there to support her did sit somewhat uncomfortably on Johnson's shoulders given she had manipulated Brandt's ex-wife into agreeing to tell her story. At least the story that Johnson had fed her.

However, any unease she had felt evaporated in the immediate aftermath. She could see that Susan felt better for doing something. Johnson may have sought to uncover and amplify her guilt, but it had definitely been there in the first place, and doing something to help the situation, as well as sharing some of the burden, had been cathartic.

In fact, the interview had gone so smoothly that Johnson had sought reassurance from Susan that she would revert to her previous position of refusing to speak to the press. It wouldn't matter that Gail had got an exclusive; journalists were like sharks and if they could sense even a drop of blood in the water they would arrive to see if there was anything left to feed on.

It wasn't just concern the media circus would return to her front door that caused Johnson to suggest Susan go and stay with friends for a while. However, she had been sufficiently emboldened by the occasion to declare that she would not be running and hiding from anyone. Johnson did little to try and convince her otherwise; if the article did provoke Brandt into returning to England, she knew who the focus of his attention would be.

Having collected the items she had gathered whilst waiting for the article to be published, Johnson had driven back to her house. For it would be here that Brandt would come first. She wondered whether he would expect to find her there and knew that would depend on how he had interpreted her actions. She was in no doubt that he would know she was behind his ex-wife speaking out. Even if it wasn't for his email revealing that he was concerned by what Johnson could ensure entered the public domain, the fact it was written by Gail, whom she had posed as when trying to bring him out into the open in Benidorm, would make the connection blindingly obvious.

The real question was what he believed her motivation to be. If he thought it was a petulant attempt to cause him pain, as some sort of revenge for him tricking her in Benidorm, then he wouldn't expect her to have moved back into her house. He would know that, whilst he remained at large, the police would have insisted she stay somewhere safe. Nevertheless, he would need to start there in order to track down her new location.

This would be the ideal situation for Johnson because she would have the element of surprise. She could just wait for him to turn up and pounce as he hunted around looking for clues as to her whereabouts.

But what she really believed was that he knew this was far more than petty point scoring. 'You know what I am capable of.' These were the last words he had sent her. A clear reference to his actions following the last newspaper article she had prompted. Brandt had warned her that any attempt to do the same would be met by similar retribution. Whilst he may have questioned her intelligence for believing she could trick him so easily, she knew that he didn't think her stupid. If nothing else, he couldn't have failed to be impressed by the apparent ease with which she had managed to track him down. It must have come as a surprise that she had seen through his elaborate plan to make it look like Franklin had fled the country alone before confessing to be the orchestrator of Brandt's actions. He would believe that she had gone to speak to his ex-wife, not only fully aware of the consequences of her actions, but perhaps even, as was the actual case, seeking to incite them.

As a result, it wouldn't make sense for her to then hide away because there was no point setting a trap which couldn't be sprung. Johnson had thought about being a little more elaborate and planting a false trail at her house that would lead him somewhere secluded. However, time had been too tight for her to find a suitable location that she could rig with the sort of traps she had in mind. Instead she thought it better to remain on familiar ground and hope that Brandt had underestimated her desire for revenge and assumed she wouldn't be there waiting for him.

The emotions her previous return to the house had provoked came flooding back as Johnson stepped into the hallway. She managed to suppress them in the knowledge that she may not be able to bring McNeil back, but at least she could make his killer pay for what he had done. She knew she had plenty of time to prepare because, if Brandt did take the bait, he would still need to travel back from wherever he was abroad, but she set about her business quickly, anxious not to allow any sense of complacency to set in.

The risk she was taking was calculated and more than once she thought about telling the police everything that had happened; reasoning with herself that, although it would certainly mean she would be whisked away to some safe-house, they could track him at the ports and there was a fair chance he could be caught as he came back into the country. But a fair chance wasn't good enough. It didn't matter to Johnson what her revelations would do to the likelihood of her being able to successfully resume her career; having twice let him slip through her fingers, she wasn't prepared for it to happen again. Moreover, this was personal, and she had a duty to see this through herself.

Parking her Audi well away from the property, she'd hefted the supplies gathered back to the house, having purchased enough food for a week because, even though she didn't expect this to take anywhere near as long, lack of preparation would not be her downfall. She set up camp in the back bedroom, thinking this would be the last place that Brandt would expect her and, of more significance, that he wouldn't fail to revisit the place where he had tied her up and sought to rape her. She tested out the floor boards on the landing to make sure she could approach him from behind in bare feet, unheard.

It saddened her to think that she wouldn't be able to inflict the sort of pain on him that he deserved. The main thing was to not present him with a situation in which he could escape. The long-bladed knife would need to be rammed into his back as soon as she got the opportunity, and she would probably need to stab it in a number of times just to be sure. She would dearly have loved to tie him up in the same way that he had done to her but her chances of physically overpowering him were slim, despite her athletic build. Nevertheless, she would make sure he knew it was her and that she was doing this, not just for all the innocent people he had murdered, but specifically for McNeil.

Johnson had bought a whole block of kitchen knives and, whilst she had kept the largest for herself to carry, she discreetly placed others round her home, including one under the pillow of her bed, in case something should go wrong. She had also planned for what to do once she had killed Brandt. Whilst she was willing to give up anything in order to act out her revenge, she wouldn't give him the satisfaction of causing her more sacrifice than was strictly necessary. She had dismissed the idea of obtaining a firearm, not just because of the difficulty getting hold of one at such short notice, but because even if she could show she had used it in self-defence, she would still be convicted of possessing one illegally. Whether that would lead to serving a prison term, given the circumstances, was debatable but one thing was certain; she would never be able to work for the police again.

Instead she would make it look like she had moved back home for no worse a reason than she naively thought herself safe with Brandt being abroad. She trusted that Susan wouldn't reveal her visit and she knew that Gail Trevelly would not want to share the credit for what was bound to be another career-defining story. She would say she was in the kitchen when Brandt entered the house and grabbed the first thing that came to hand; claiming that she had tried to hide but fled upstairs, and it was only her decision to go into the spare room rather than her own bedroom that saved her. She knew she would have to answer questions like why she didn't go out the front door when she ran and, although she didn't expect to convince everybody, the main thing was that she had a plausible story that would be impossible to disprove. All she needed to do once she had killed Brandt was stuff the rest of her supplies in a kitchen cupboard and run around to collect up the remainder of the knives.

With everything ready and it still being only lunchtime on the first day of the printing of the newspaper article, Johnson got a few hours' sleep on her spare bed whilst she had the chance. After that, she would rely on her determination, as well as energy drinks, to keep her alert until she came face to face with her nemesis once more.

Chapter Thirty-three

Brandt drove up the street that held so many memories despite only being there once before. His speed was neither fast nor slow, just what would be considered normal. As far as he could tell, there were no unmarked police cars parked in any of the locations he would have expected. He hadn't anticipated finding any, but it paid to be careful. Just as he had known Johnson was acting alone when he saw her on the beach, so too was this all her own doing – the police would not have allowed her to be in the line of fire again. As he passed the property, he could see no signs of life but felt sure that if she wasn't in there, at least she was expecting him to visit to try and find clues as to her whereabouts. Why else would she have sought to provoke him like that? It hadn't been enough to get Susan to sell her story to the newspaper; she had got her to tell vicious lies about their marriage. It had to have served a purpose. Brandt had no idea what he may find in the house, but if there was a trap then he hadn't come all this way not to spring it.

Turning around in a side road much further up, he switched off the lights as he came back down the street. He needed to park close to the house and was grateful that his petrol hybrid Volvo XC90 was nice and quiet. It was a coincidence that he had managed to find such an appropriate vehicle, because his main objective at the service station north of Paris had been to find someone who looked similar to him. It may have been the same trick he had used with Franklin in order to get out of the country but, with Johnson not acting in an official capacity, the last thing the authorities would have been expecting was for him to re-enter England.

With plenty of people returning from their summer holidays, he'd had enough to choose from and it was a simple process once he had spotted a suitable target. Unsurprisingly the man had not been alone, but Brandt was grateful that there wasn't the complication of him having children in tow. Brandt had simply sat at one of the outside benches, apparently enjoying the sunshine, whilst he waited for the man and his wife to go inside and complete their business. They had only been in there for a few minutes before both emerged clutching takeaway coffees. Finding somewhere sensible to place them on entering their vehicle, would prove something of a distraction. And Brandt had only needed the briefest of seconds.

It had been simple and if any of the other motorists had observed Brandt following them and getting into the back, they would have seen nothing amiss. He had opened his door at the same time as the driver had shut his, so as to mask the sound. They were not aware of his presence until he leaned forward to put the large knife to the wife's throat. That was how they had driven off, with Brandt sipping the man's coffee, and enjoying the taste despite it having been made with milk; directing them to a secluded spot where he didn't even bothered to tie up the wife, whilst he put the man in the boot. He had seen many frightened people over his career and had always been a good judge of character. There was more chance of her sprouting wings and flying off than there was her electing

222

to run and leave her husband behind. Besides, Brandt had sounded so reassuring as he explained that he simply needed a ride home and that he was popping the man into the ample-sized boot, just until they had cleared customs in France. To add to the subterfuge, he had her remain in the passenger seat and had called out things like 'I hope that's not too tight' and 'nod if the gag's making it hard for you to breathe' whilst supposedly fixing the man's bonds; all the while smiling whilst watching his eyes bulge in horror as his life blood drained out from the wide gash to his throat.

It hadn't surprised Brandt that neither of them recognised him because that just summed up society as far as he was concerned. Living in West London and not fitting the profile of any of his victims, he doubted they had given the news of his exploits more than a second glance. In fact, the wife had remained so compliant that he had even taken the risk of pulling up to a passport window on the passenger's side. The British attendant had given Brandt the merest of glances before asking him to open the back windows. With the now familiar procedure out of the way, they sailed through customs and Brandt's wait for the train was much calmer than last time.

The woman had seemed to believe the best course of action was to say as little as possible, but he had coaxed her into conversation to help while away the time until they boarded, and during the short journey back to Folkestone. Her reticence soon faded and, the more she spoke, the more he found he quite liked her. Brandt wouldn't have described her as attractive but her somewhat plain features, complemented by a thoroughly drab brown ponytail, kind of suited her. What impressed him most was that she made no effort to appeal to his humanity by talking about family or what an important job both she and her husband did. She merely gave honest answers to his simple questions and he appreciated having finally found a woman that didn't seem to want to play games.

It was therefore with regret that he pulled off the motorway almost as soon as they joined it after arriving at Folkestone, and found the same rutted entrance to the field along the empty single-track road. He had kept his promise to reunite the couple and even allowed her to open the boot to reveal her husband, causing her to believe that he was about to hot foot it into the nearest field and they would be able to continue on their journey otherwise unimpeded. Brandt had watched with interest as it took her brain a while to process the sight before her. Any compassion he had felt was gone as he drank in the moment; even allowing her to air the screams that followed before running the sharp blade expertly across her throat.

As Brandt sat outside DCI Johnson's house, he thought that there could be far worse ways to meet one's death. With the couple still in their final embrace mere feet behind him, he fished out his phone. He would send the text before getting out of the car. He couldn't see Johnson looking out of her window but, just in case, it should prove an ample distraction.

As with his driving up the road earlier, he exited the XC90 neither quickly nor slowly and walked calmly up the short path to her door. For the benefit of any neighbours who might be watching, he moved his fist back and forth, pretending to knock.

Chapter Thirty-four

The incoming text message startled Johnson. She must have drifted off. It was more than a day since she had taken advantage of finishing her preparations by allowing herself a few hours' sleep. She had awoken on that occasion to find confirmation that Brandt had read the article and, more significantly, the implication that he was coming to get her. With air travel out of the question she guessed it would easily take him the best part of a day to get back to England, which meant he could well be in the country by now and she would know in the next 48 hours whether her plan had worked. Having allowed her body to betray her so early on, even if she had only been dozing for a few moments, was unacceptable to Johnson. Her irritation was such that she nearly forgot the thing that had roused her and almost absentmindedly opened her phone.

A spike of adrenaline ran through her veins as she saw that the message was from him. But its contents confused her.

> *– I warned you what would happen.*

The message was exactly the same as before and she scrolled down to look at the previous one to confirm that her mind wasn't playing tricks. What did that mean? Was he having trouble making his way back into the country and wanted to remind her? Or was it just an empty threat and he was sunning himself somewhere; hoping to apply what little pressure he could?

It was then that she noticed the symbol indicating that there was a photo attached. Upon returning to her house she hadn't thought to connect her new phone to the Wi-Fi connection and had been relying on her cellular data, which had the setting whereby it wouldn't automatically download large files.

It was more with curiosity than fear that she clicked the icon to reveal the attachment. It soon changed as she observed a gagged and clearly terrified Susan. The writing at the bottom intensified the horror.

> *— If you're not here within an hour or I even suspect the police are coming, she dies. That'll make it 2 deaths you are responsible for.*

Johnson sat there, stunned. How could she have got this so wrong? Again! It made sense that his primary target would be his wife. He would believe her responsible for the suffering that had led to him becoming a killer. It mattered not that he would see her as being put up to accepting the interview by Johnson; the fact remained that she had been the one who made those enormously disparaging comments. That he could then use the situation to take out the other thorn in his side was just a bonus to him, which is what his message had meant all along. It wasn't so much of a threat as a plea to not get Susan involved.

Johnson gagged and brought up her meagre lunch of baked beans and tinned fruit, which she had ironically selected as they weren't likely to create enough of a smell to give away her location in the house. But the stench now it had been regurgitated and was splashed over the bedroom floor, caused her to retch once more.

She wiped away the involuntary tears and tried to get up from her crouched position. A voice in her head was screaming at her that being a vigilante had only ever served to fuck things up more than they already were, and that she needed to phone the police immediately. But Brandt had been crystal clear: '...I even suspect the police are coming she dies.'

An hour didn't give her long either. With her foot down, she estimated that it would still take her 45 minutes, so she couldn't allow indecision to cost this innocent woman her life. She would just have to think in the car and work out how to approach this. Tucking the large blade into the back of her waistband, Johnson ran towards the main bedroom, retrieved the small paring knife from under her pillow and slid it into her sock as she raced down the stairs; cursing herself once more. All that planning, and she had been so wide of the mark again. If Brandt's actions following the first newspaper article hadn't been enough of a lesson, how easily he had played her in Benidorm should have been.

As she reached for the front door she was put in mind of the proverb: Fool me once, shame on you; fool me twice, shame on me. With the latch opening in her hand she wondered where she had read it.

She didn't get to complete the thought.

Former Detective Superintendent Jeffrey Brandt was stood before her.

Chapter Thirty-five

Johnson's first moment of consciousness was a sense that she had experienced this before. That was the sum total of the feeling and without any context as to what this was. It occurred to her more as a statement of fact but, as she attempted to explore the sensation, she came to understand that it hadn't been good. Not that she knew why.

She appreciated a choice had to be made because her current state did not represent an existence; merely the gap between two worlds. Johnson wanted to make the decision based on knowledge of the implication of each path but, equally, she knew that to establish the environment of either world was to effectively make that choice.

So, she waited. Unable to shake the belief that either path spelled danger, Johnson started to consider who she was. She grasped at brief snatches of memory, attempting to piece them together to get an awareness of her self. This was far from easy because the fragments were disparate, but she had a logical mind and eventually found ways in which they might fit.

It was then that part of her mind spoke to her, and warned her off what she was doing. It told her that to continue to fight against her current state of being would lead to suffering. But she didn't like this voice, believing its origin was cowardice and its claims duplicitous. Johnson had already inferred from her splinters of memory that she was a strong woman and so the person in her head must be an unwanted intruder. As a consequence, her seeking to regain genuine consciousness became as much of an act of defiance as a search for truth.

As Johnson grappled with the purpose of her existence, two things became clear to her. She felt both pain and love. Trying to separate them in order to examine them better, she found that they were more than entwined; one did not function in her without the other. With the voice now screaming at her to stop, she explored this peculiar symbiotic relationship and slowly the context for these emotions was revealed.

McNeil. A man. A man she cared for. A man who had caused her pain.

Johnson attempted to focus McNeil. She couldn't pinpoint anything specifically. She knew she found him attractive but accepted that her feelings weren't based on physical form. But as she tried to explore his spiritual being, she was unable to prevent an examination of the pain. McNeil lived, but only inside her because, in the real world, he had died.

The real world. She considered what that was and, more importantly, why McNeil didn't exist in it anymore.

In the same instant she realised she had inadvertently chosen a path. Johnson opened her eyes. In the fraction of a second it had taken to do this, she had worked out that it was highly probable her hands would be bound. They were, but behind her back rather than to her bed frame. Nor was she lying down but was sat on one of her kitchen chairs. What's more, and with great relief, she was fully clothed. This had not been anticipated, but thoughts of its strangeness evaporated when a man walked from behind her and sat in the chair opposite.

'Hello, Miss Johnson, I expected you to have more of a tan from your recent holiday.' The observation was conversational, but mirth danced in Brandt's eyes.

'Your… your wife…' She spluttered, total recall and its harsh reality having set in.

He laughed; cruel and mocking. 'I know you like to play games, so I thought you might appreciate this one.'

'I don't… I don't understand. The photo…' Perhaps it had been a hoax in order to lure her out. If it was, then he had succeeded. If Susan was unharmed then Johnson felt she could better meet her own fate.

'Don't worry, it's old,' he responded, deriving huge pleasure from the hope he saw etched across her face. 'Well, when I say old,' he continued theatrically, looking at his watch, 'it's probably about four hours old now.'

'She's…?'

'Indeed,' he replied with false solemnity. 'But before you go blaming yourself, let's just say she probably had it coming.' Johnson started retching again, unconsciously trying to bring her hands up to cover her mouth. Her bonds were tight. Brandt observed her with curiosity, as though considering whether it was part of some act.

'Finished?' he asked with an arched eyebrow, unable to hide his distaste at the saliva running down her chin. 'If it's any consolation, she didn't seem that surprised to see me. Whatever you said to convince her to betray me, she knew what the consequence would be. In a way I kind of admire that. Don't do the crime if you can't do the time.' He shrugged as though that somehow justified his actions. 'But what I don't understand is that you looked genuinely shocked to see me. How can that be so? It's not as though I hadn't warned you. Or am I just misreading the situation and you are surprised to find yourself tied up again?' He tutted good naturedly. 'You really do have an over-inflated ego DCI Johnson, and to think I thought our fun and games on the beach would have taught you a little more humility.'

Johnson didn't consider Brandt's jibes; she was still trying to process that Susan was dead. Had she really expected him to confront her? Why hadn't she agreed to go and stay with family? With Johnson not there in an official capacity and therefore unable to offer her somewhere anonymous, she knew he would be able to track her down and would therefore be endangering others. Perhaps she had hoped that he would see it as too risky with the reporters camped outside, but even Johnson knew that he would simply have to approach from the back garden and merely wait until she came outside for a cigarette.

'What do you mean, don't go blaming yourself?'

'She told me about your conversation. She told me how you had made her feel guilty for my actions; that she had needed to try and put things right.' He sighed. 'I think she wanted me to tell her that she wasn't responsible.' A long pause. 'I didn't, of course,' he smirked.

'You, sick bastard.'

The words had barely escaped her mouth when Brandt lunged forward, grabbing her shoulders; his face now inches from hers. 'I was compassionate. I wasn't going to lie to her like you did but I didn't seek to prove to her that the awful things she said about my... my capability weren't true.' He took a deep breath, withdrawing slightly. 'Don't you judge me, you fucking bitch. You caused this. You didn't stick to the rules! It was fine to hunt me, that was part of the game, but as soon as you cheated, you ruined things for both of us.'

'What are you going to do to me?'

'See, there you go again. It's all about you, isn't it?! You couldn't accept that I was better than you and that you were unable to catch me. You provoked me, knowing what I was capable of, and you couldn't accept the consequences. Your colleague... your lover died because of you.'

231

'Don't you fucking dare talk about him!' she roared, rage coming to the fore.

Brandt sat back, clearly startled but otherwise unaffected. 'Look, if it's any consolation, I didn't mean to kill him.' The reasonableness to his tone only angered Johnson further. 'But the point I'm making is that you didn't then learn your lesson. It's not as though I expected you to leave it altogether, but I thought you would stick to the rules again and follow procedure.' He shrugged. 'I do take my share of the responsibility. I let you get away with what you tried to do in Benidorm. I knew I shouldn't but... let's just say I was a little preoccupied by other events. However, whilst they weren't strictly my fault, what happened with Trish certainly wasn't yours.' He sat back, folding his arms, clearly coming to some form of conclusion. 'Therefore, I suppose it would be fair to say we are both responsible for what happened to my wife.'

'I don't give a fuck about your wife,' Johnson spat. All McNeil's sister's words at the funeral had done was uncover the simple truth. A truth that she could only see in its entirety now. Revenge was all that mattered to her now; it was all she had left.

The horror on Brandt's face matched her own. What had she become? But whatever it was, she wasn't prepared to face that now because, sitting before her, was the man responsible for her gruesome transformation. All it made her realise was that the fear she harboured was pointless. It didn't matter what he did to her; he had killed her, the real her, the moment he had plunged his knife into McNeil. Her physical body may have remained but what had been inside, her very being, had been ripped out.

'You didn't just take away the man I cared for, you took away my capacity to love,' she whispered with tears of despair streaming down her face. Johnson wasn't so much looking at Brandt, more through him and to the emptiness that lay beyond. She barely noticed him lean forward until he raised his arm. She believed for a moment that he was going to put it around her, to seek somehow to provide comfort. But the speed at which it shot forward dispelled that thought, even before she noticed that his hand had become a fist.

Chapter Thirty-six

This time there was no limbo for Johnson. Instead there was the immediate transition from no thought or feeling to consciousness. It was a sloshing sound that had awoken her, but that sense was soon overtaken by the pungent stench of petrol. She swung her head round in panic; her earlier conclusions of the pointlessness of her continued existence replaced by the body's baser instinct of self-preservation.

She tried to cry out as Brandt walked calmly past her to complete the circle of liquid on the floor. 'Shh, no more talking,' he said soothingly, opening the back door to toss the metal container far into the garden. 'We both knew it would come to this.'

The full reality of the situation came to Johnson even before he picked up a new jerrycan and held it aloft. Instinctively she closed her eyes, awaiting the stinging shock of petrol on her face. It didn't come, and she eventually opened them to find Brandt maintaining the same position as before. A few moments passed with them both staring at each other before he started tipping the contents over his own head.

His involuntary gasps subsided. 'You questioned whether I could be intimate with a woman. But what I have learned is that death is a far more intimate experience than sex.'

Despite her terror, Johnson found herself remembering the tenderness of the moment she had shared with McNeil as they held hands whilst the blood drained from him.

'There are many layers to its intimacy. I used to fantasise about plunging off a cliff and for my body to be dashed on the rocks below, but now I have created death I can see it is a better experience shared. And what could be more intimate than dying together?'

Brandt smiled, a broad warm smile that told Johnson any hatred he had for her had gone. He marched past her. 'Now where did I leave that lighter?' he asked with a casualness she found more chilling than anything he had said or done before.

Moments later she heard the loud whoomph of fuel being ignited, followed by screaming. Feeling intense heat behind her, she noticed the air rushing past her to fill the vacuum being created by the oxygen that had already been burned. Then she saw the flames dancing across the liquid either side of her, coming to meet in the middle. With the brightness now in her kitchen blinding her and her lungs already struggling to breathe effectively, she started bucking in her chair. Johnson knew there was every chance her actions would cause her to tip into the fire that surrounded her, but she had little option unless she wanted to wait until the intense heat caused her clothes to catch light.

Suddenly she could feel movement; small but definitely there. She contorted her left hand in an attempt to try and exploit it, whilst expecting the action to cause her bonds to tighten. They didn't, and she could feel the rope loosen further. A moment later her hand was free. Instantly she started yanking at her right wrist. Her finger picked and pulled indiscriminately until that arm was released too. In the instant euphoria that followed she tried to stand and, instead, plunged forward through the flames and out the other side. She quickly pulled up her legs to take them away from the immediate danger but, with them still bound, it only served to drag the chair into the fire. Johnson's screams as it caught light stopped as she observed the metal object glinting. It was the small paring knife she had placed in her sock before answering the door. Brandt must have either failed to notice it or had not thought it sufficiently important to remove it.

She reached for it and fought her natural instinct to immediately pull her hand away. Through gritted teeth and eyes unable not to see the skin blistering on the back of her hand, she grabbed the knife, grateful that its metal hilt hadn't heated up too much yet to hold. Hitching in what little oxygen her lungs could find in the air that remained in the kitchen she slashed at her bonds, hardly noticing the cuts she inflicted on her ankles.

Finally free of the chair, Johnson crawled to the back door, with coughs now wracking her body. Wrenching it open, she threw herself forward against the cool air being sucked past her. She could smell her hair sizzling and proceeded to roll off the patio and onto the grass. Coming to a stop she barely processed the sight of the dark form of a body silhouetted on the kitchen floor before she closed her eyes against the fragments of glass that flew in her direction from the back windows being blown out.

The voice was back again, telling her to just lie there and allow the blissfulness of oblivion to take away her pain. Johnson no longer found that voice deceitful, only caring. The temptation was heightened by the heat that was now intolerable. But she knew what to agree would mean. Whether despite or in spite of Brandt, she wanted to live, and summoning the last of her strength as well as her will, she hauled herself up onto her knees and crawled to the relative safety of the overgrown flowerbed at the back of her garden, where she finally allowed herself to pass out.

She may not have noticed the explosion that followed the contents of her gas boiler being ignited but Brandt did. He had stopped at the junction to find the switch for the Volvo's heated seats, in the hope that it might help to dry his soaking wet clothes. Looking back up the road at the ball of flame rising to disappear into the night sky, in the same way as he had chosen not to twist the knife in Sarah Donovan, he hoped that he had sufficiently loosened Johnson's bonds for her to be able to escape. Happy that he was leaving Nottingham under better circumstances than a fortnight earlier, he switched on the radio and began whistling along to the anonymous tune, and turned his thoughts to how he was going to dispose of the lone body that remained in the boot.

If you enjoyed this book, please let others know by leaving a quick review on Amazon. Also, if you spot anything untoward in the paperback, get in touch. We strive for the best quality and appreciate reader feedback.

editor@thebookfolks.com

www.thebookfolks.com

Book I, available on Kindle and in paperback.

He spent his life fighting crime. Now he has a taste for it himself. His first attack is a stab in the dark. Next time, he'll kill. Knowing how the police work, ex-cop Jeffrey Brandt stays one step ahead of them. He will even taunt those trying to catch him. DCI Stella Johnson is responsible for finding him. Has she got what it takes?

Book III, coming soon on Kindle and in paperback.

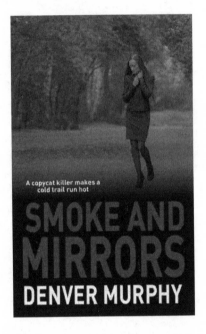

A copycat killer makes a
cold trail run hot

SMOKE AND
MIRRORS

DENVER MURPHY

Has Brandt's killing spree come to an end? Is it over? Or
have his actions spawned something worse? Will DCI
Johnson get her revenge, or will she fall victim to her own
rage?

Made in the USA
Lexington, KY
10 March 2019